awakening

chasing yesterday

book one
awakening

robin wasserman

SCHOLASTIC INC.

New York Toronto London Auckland Sydney
Mexico City New Delhi Hong Kong Buenos Aires

No part of this publication may be reproduced, stored in a retrieval system, or transmitted in any form or by any means, electronic, mechanical, photocopying, recording, or otherwise, without written permission of the publisher. For information regarding permission, write to Scholastic Inc., Attention: Permissions Department, 557 Broadway, New York, NY 10012.

ISBN-13: 978-0-439-93338-4
ISBN-10: 0-439-93338-2

Copyright © 2007 by Robin Wasserman

Book design by Tim Hall

12 11 10 9 8 7 6 5 4 3 2   7 8 9 10 11 12/0
                                        40

Printed in the U.S.A.
First printing, May 2007

For Susie

found

Light swallowed the darkness.

She must have opened her eyes.

At first, there was nothing but the pain. It began as a low rumble, background noise. It was almost soothing, the way it folded around her like a blanket. It made her mind dull, gave her a place to hide. It throbbed. It hummed. It came in waves, tossing her up, dragging her under, washing over her, carrying her away from herself, from everything.

But it was growing. Swelling. The rumble turned into a roar. The pain stopped cradling her, began clawing at her, devouring her. It was like a living beast, ripping her apart from the inside, struggling to break free to the outside world. The darkness nipped at the edges of her mind, crawling back, offering her peace, a sleep free of pain.

And she almost accepted.

Instead, she screamed.

Or she tried to. It came out as a moan. But it was enough. The tiniest of motions — opening her mouth, drawing in a breath, tipping her head back to unleash the sound — sent a new, different kind of pain screaming through her. It was sudden and sharp, a knife slicing across her chest. It cut through the dull fog of her mind. The bright light of the world resolved itself into defined shapes, sharp lines.

She was awake.

And, for the first time, she was afraid.

The light . . . she realized it was the sun, blazing through a haze of acrid gray smoke. It hurt to squint. It hurt more to look away. She lay on her back, her arms stretched out to her sides. Beneath her, the ground felt hard, uneven. Small, sharp objects bored into her back, biting into her skin. Somehow, they made everything real. She was afraid of floating into the darkness again — but they kept her on the ground.

She couldn't move her head, but she darted her eyes from side to side. Nothing. Nothing but pitted gray cement, smoke, and blue sky.

Where am I? she thought, her breath rasping as she sucked in more air. There was a tickle at the back of her mind, like a voice she could just barely hear. The answer was there, just beyond her reach. But when she strained for it, the pain came back worse than before.

Maybe this was all a dream, she decided.

So she lay still, breathed, and waited to wake up.

At first, she thought she was imagining him. Shadows flickered at the corners of her eyes — motion, where before there had been only stillness. She thought he was a phantom and waited for him to disappear.

Instead, he approached. Slowly, like she was a wild animal, like she would bite. Like she could move.

He was just a silhouette against the sun, his face hidden in shadow. She knew he was coming for her, and she should have felt relieved. But as he stepped closer, she saw his shoes, black leather with shiny gold bars where the laces should be. And she screamed.

Panic.

Terror swept through her, without reason and without end. She needed to stand, to run, to escape. *Now*, her body told her. But she couldn't catch her breath; she couldn't stop shaking.

And she couldn't run away — she couldn't even sit up. She was too weak.

She was too terrified.

I can't stop him. She didn't know where the thought had come from, what it meant, or why she felt so certain it was true. *He'll take me back there.* It made no sense. Stop him from what? Take her where?

It's all over now. The voice in her mind was her own, but it knew more than she did, and it was afraid.

The man drew closer, circling cautiously, almost as if *he* were the one afraid of *her.* Her muscles tensed and she opened her mouth, but her throat closed up. She couldn't make a sound. The dark figure was almost on her.

Then, without warning, the scream of a siren cut through the silence — and the man ran away.

She never saw his face.

Now there were people everywhere, and light and noise. And more pain. The man from the ambulance lifted her arms, squeezed her wrist; another shined a flashlight into her eyes. She was poked and prodded, a blanket laid over her body, a mask pressed against her mouth. She panicked as the thick plastic covered her face, but her next breath was deep and fresh, and it gave her the strength to take another.

4

Warm hands gripped her on either side, lifted her up, then placed her down on a long, smooth board. They laid thick straps across her body, tied her down.

Trapped! The panic was back.

"No," she whispered, forcing her mouth to form the word. "*No.*"

But the straps clicked shut, were pulled tight. A hand pressed softly against her forehead. She felt herself lifting off the ground, then moving forward, toward the gaping mouth of a white truck. Its sirens flashed, turning the world red, then blue, then red again.

"Shhh, it's going to be all right," a man said — and somehow she knew it wasn't the dark figure she'd seen before. He was gone. For now. "Do you know what happened?" he asked, leaning over her. His eyebrows were bushy, his eyes deep green. They crinkled at the corners as he tried to smile. "Can you tell us your name?"

He lifted the mask so she could speak.

"Do you know who you are, hon?" he asked as, in the distance, an engine roared to life. A door slammed shut, and the ambulance lurched into motion. "Do you know your name?"

Of course she did.

It was . . .

She was . . .

But where there should have been a name, a person, a life, an answer, there was nothing. Her mind was black. Empty.

"I don't know," she whispered. The words scraped her throat raw. "I don't know who I am."

And the darkness returned.

trapped

The pain woke her up.

Cold steel pressed against her back. Above her was a gray ceiling, flecked with spots of black. A bag of pink liquid hung above her head, and a long, thin line stretched from it to a patch of white gauze on her left arm. She could see the pink liquid dripping out of the bag, through the tube, disappearing beneath the gauze. Disappearing into her body.

Go, she thought. *Get out. Now.*

She struggled to sit up, but something held her back, tied her to the long slab of cold metal. She was chained like an animal, her wrists and ankles bound by fleece-lined leather bracelets. They were soft, cozy, didn't dig into her skin no matter how much she strained. But they were still chains.

She was still a prisoner.

She jerked her arms, kicked her legs, pulled, tugged, grunted with effort as she struggled to escape. She opened her mouth, expecting that, as in her dreams, nothing would come out. Instead, she screamed. Howled in pain and frustration and fear.

And they came running.

Two men, dressed in white. One stood by her feet, and she tried to kick the knowing smile off his face, but the leather cuffs held her down. He nodded. The other man drew out a syringe of clear liquid. The needle was two inches long and gleamed in the light.

"Nooooooo!" She struggled to escape it. The smiling man pressed a hand against her to keep her still; she could feel his fingers boring into her. The other man injected his needle into the thin plastic tubing and stepped back.

"You'll feel better soon," he told her. Now he smiled, too.

"Why?" she asked. "Why are you doing this to . . . ?" But her voice trailed off. Suddenly, the question didn't seem important anymore. Nor did the men. So much easier to stare up at the ceiling, which was rippling like a pool of water. So much easier to stop struggling and just float, watching the world swirl around her. She forgot about the men, about the needle, about everything, and gazed up at the soft pink liquid above her, dripping down into her, nourishing her. She felt like she was falling into a cloud of pink. "So soft," she whispered happily, her heavy eyes drifting shut. "So pretty . . ."

She didn't hear the men leave or the door shut behind them. And she didn't start screaming again until she'd fallen asleep.

"Are you going to be a good girl now?" the nurse asked, her hand hesitating over the leather straps.

She nodded. It made her dizzy.

"And you understand where you are?" the woman prompted her.

"In a hospital," she said quietly. "I got hurt."

No one would tell her any more than that. And she still couldn't remember.

The woman, almost as wide as she was tall, with curly red hair and a large mole on her left cheek, patted her shoulder. She tried not to jerk away. "You'll be okay, honey. Don't you worry."

And, as promised, the leather straps slid open and she was free.

She could have run — but where would she go?

"They thought you were going to hurt yourself, sweetie," the nurse said, sliding a tray of food in front of her. "That's the only reason they had you held down like that. But you're not going to hurt anyone, isn't that right?"

She nodded, like a good girl.

"I told 'em so." The woman checked her clipboard, then played with the nozzle on one of the plastic bags hanging over the bed.

A tube still fed into her arm. The pink liquid still dripped, slow and steady.

"You were just scared, that's all. Little girl like you, all alone, a big explosion like that, of course you were scared." The woman slapped a black cuff around her arm, sealed it shut with Velcro, and began to pump. The cuff got tighter and tighter, until the pressure was almost unbearable. But just when she thought she couldn't take it anymore, when she thought she would need to scream again — even if it meant more chains, more drugs, more sleep — the pressure disappeared. And the woman took the cuff off and scribbled something down on her board.

Just checking my blood pressure, she thought, then started in surprise. How had she known that?

"Just try to eat something, hon, and the doctor will be in soon."

She stared down at the tray in front of her. There was a small plastic cup of yellowish-orange juice. A dinner roll covered in plastic wrap. And a bowl of brownish-orange mash that smelled like feet.

"What's the matter?" the nurse asked. "Don't you like macaroni and cheese?"

"I . . ."

But she didn't know. She couldn't remember having eaten it before, just like she couldn't remember anything else.

Suddenly, she wasn't very hungry.

She was bruised everywhere, and it still hurt to move. But she was strong enough to get out of bed and walk to the mirror. She stood there, staring at the stranger trapped behind the glass. When she touched her face, the girl in the mirror touched her face, too.

That's me, she told herself. It didn't seem possible.

The girl in the mirror looked thirteen or fourteen. But that didn't matter. Her real age could be measured in hours: forty-eight.

It had been two days since she had opened her

eyes to find herself on the ground, in pain, alone. And before that, there was nothing but a blank. As if she had never existed.

"I don't understand," she said, avoiding Dr. Fisher's eyes. "I can remember how to walk and talk." She pointed at her dinner tray. "I can remember that this is a cup and this is a plate — I can remember what a hospital is and what a doctor does. *So why can't I remember my own name?*"

Dr. Fisher, the neurologist, was a handsome man in his thirties, so tall he nearly had to bend his head to come into the room.

He sat down next to her bed. "The memory's a funny thing," he told her. "The brain stores its memories in a lot of different ways. There's procedural memory — that's how your body remembers to do things like walk or breathe or play the piano. And semantic memory — that's names of things. Facts. It's how you know who the president is and that dogs have four legs and a tail. Then there's episodic memory, which the brain seems to store in an entirely different way. It's how you know yourself — all the things that have happened to you, who you love, what you fear. It's all the things that make you who you are."

"All the things I can't remember."

He began to pat her on the shoulder, then stopped, remembering that she was still covered in bruises. "You know, in a way, you're lucky."

"Yeah, right," she said bitterly. "I'm really lucky." She had been hearing the refrain all day. Such a massive explosion, and yet she had emerged with nothing more than some bruises and a concussion.

And a gaping black hole in her mind that had devoured her entire life.

"You can still function," Dr. Fisher pointed out. "You can still speak. You can remember enough to interact with the outside world. That's luckier than a lot of people. And even episodic memory damage could have been worse."

She didn't say anything, but she didn't believe him. What could be worse than lying there a stranger to herself, trapped in a body she didn't recognize?

"At any rate," he continued, "we've been unable to find an underlying physical cause. Your memory loss seems — and this is a good thing — purely psychological."

"So it's all in my head?" she asked sourly. "I'm just crazy?"

"No," he said quickly. "I would never say that. It's

common for physical or emotional trauma to cause this kind of memory blackout — we call it retrograde amnesia. Of course, it's not often this severe, but . . ." A frown flickered across his face, then quickly disappeared. "We still have every reason to believe that it's temporary."

"And what if it's not?"

He stood up abruptly, and when he spoke again, his back was to her so she couldn't see his face. "Just relax," he said. "Try not to worry about it. The memories will come back — it just may take some time."

But she felt like time was running out. She told him so, just before he stepped out the door. He paused for a moment and turned back, flashing his bright white smile. "You're in a scary place, surrounded by strangers, and you're still in shock," he said. "Your body is still on guard — it still thinks trouble is on its way. But the trouble is behind you now, Jane. You're safe." And then he walked away.

They all called her Jane.

Jane Doe.

She didn't feel like a Jane. Of course, she didn't feel like the "poor, lost child" they were talking about on TV, either.

"The mysterious explosion took down almost

three city blocks, but claimed only a single victim," the blond-haired woman on Channel 5 said, pursing her lips like she thought the explosion should have tried harder. "Found unconscious a hundred yards from the center of the explosion, Jane Doe is now in stable condition at St. Anthony's Hospital, where doctors expect her to make a full recovery."

"Sources tell us that Jane Doe still has no memory of who she is or what she was doing in an area containing little but vacant lots and empty warehouses," said the woman on Channel 7 with the shiny brown hair and orange lips. "Authorities ask anyone who has knowledge of her identity to please come forward." And a picture of *her* — of Jane Doe — would flash on the screen. She remembered having the picture taken, sitting up in the hospital bed, holding herself still and wondering if she was expected to smile. But the face on the television screen seemed no more familiar than the face in the mirror. A pale wraith in a hospital gown with a white bandage taped to her forehead. Her mouth was a wavy line, as if the camera had caught her lips mid-tremble.

The girl looked like a Jane Doe.

But she doesn't look like me.

Whoever that was.

The woman on Channel 2 had short, curly hair the color of dirt. "I'm broadcasting live from the site of the explosion," she said, clutching the microphone and grinning at the camera. Her red dress was the only blotch of color on the screen; she was surrounded by a sea of grayish brown, twisted metal, broken boards, and rubble.

Wreckage.

"Sources say that an abandoned cache of flammable chemicals was stored in the basement of the building that used to stand behind me," she said, gesturing to the scorched heap. "But authorities have yet to determine what caused them to ignite." She put on her sad face. "Authorities are also still searching for information about the poor child found amid the rubble, the *Girl without a Past*. We're all pulling for that brave little girl to find her way home."

The woman disappeared from the screen, replaced by a man behind a news desk. His face looked like it had been molded out of plastic, with a wave of blond hair painted across the top. "It's a sad, sad thing," he said, shaking his head. Then his white teeth flashed. "But what's not so sad is our weekend weather forecast — looks like sunny days are here again!"

She turned off the television.

smile

It was better not to sleep.

When sleep came, so did the dreams.

She didn't remember them, but she woke up screaming. Sweating. Crying. And terrified.

She wouldn't let herself be afraid during the day. She was no little girl lost; she was no victim.

But at night, it was harder to be brave — and there was no one to pretend for.

Sometimes, when she forced herself to stay awake, there were no dreams, there was just the music, an off-key melody that seemed more familiar than anything else — and played only in her head. She knew because she asked a night nurse, "Where's that music coming from?"

The nurse looked at her like she was crazy.

She hadn't asked again.

Crazy or no, the music was the closest thing she

had to a memory, a clue to her past. It only lasted for a minute or two. But after an hour it came back. A few hours later, it came back again. Soft, haunting notes that made her feel lost in her own body, like she was watching herself from very far away.

Maybe it was a song her mother used to sing her.

Maybe it was just the morphine.

"What do you mean you're releasing me?" she demanded. "You haven't cured me yet."

Dr. Fisher bit his lip and rubbed a hand through his scruffy hair. "It's not quite that simple, Jane —"

"Stop calling me that!" she cried. The name felt like a lie. Worse, it felt like a submission. She was sick of waiting patiently for someone to figure out what was wrong. To *fix* her. It obviously wasn't going to happen — so maybe she needed to start fixing things herself.

Dr. Fisher leaned against the cabinet where patients were supposed to store their belongings. Hers was empty. "What would you like me to call you?"

She glared at him. He didn't look away. "I don't know," she finally admitted. Dr. Fisher wasn't the enemy. *She* was the enemy, at war with her own mind. And so far, she was losing.

He sighed. "Except for some bruising and the memory loss, you're perfectly healthy," he said. "And as I've already explained, in your situation, a temporary loss of memory isn't that unusual."

"And you're *sure* it's temporary?"

Instead of answering, he slapped a large, translucent sheet of plastic onto a lighted screen. "This is a scan of your brain," he said. "And while there are some . . . irregularities, there's no physical damage. None."

"Irregularities?"

"It's nothing," he said quickly. "Everyone's brain chemistry is slightly different, and yours has some elevated levels of . . . well, it's just boring medical jargon. Nothing that would interest you, trust me." He laughed but stopped abruptly when he realized he was laughing alone.

She pointed at a small gray smudge toward the right side of the scan. "So what's that?"

He grinned. "Good eye. As far as I can tell, that's some kind of hearing aid that was probably implanted when you were a kid. It's a fairly unusual device — we're actually hoping it might be able to help us track down where you came from. Medical records are a pretty good way of doing that. But in the meantime . . ."

"In the meantime, you're sending me away." It

wasn't that she wanted to stay in the hospital, but at least it was a place she knew. It was the *only* place she knew.

"Jane, I know you think we haven't done enough for you, but I promise, your best hope now is time," Dr. Fisher said. "There's no reason yet to opt for more . . . drastic treatment methods." The thin lines around his mouth and eyes deepened, making him look much older. "The brain is an amazing thing, and in cases like this, it usually heals itself. Your memories may return to you all at once, or they may come back in flashes. Sometimes seeing familiar people or places can jolt you into remembering, so hopefully, they'll be able to track down your family soon. And you'll still be getting regular checkups, just to make sure . . ." His voice trailed off.

"What?"

This time, he did look away. "Well, as I say, we're pretty sure that your mind just needs a little time to heal. But, sometimes after a head trauma . . . Well, we just want to make sure we didn't miss anything and that no new problems arise. So if you start experiencing any strange symptoms — dizziness, pain, hallucinations — make sure you let someone know, okay?"

She nodded, wondering whether to tell him about the dreams. And the music.

"But don't worry. I'm sure you're going to be fine. Just give it some time."

"It's not like I have much of a choice," she said, finally rewarding him with a smile. They both laughed, even though it wasn't particularly funny.

"We'll miss you around here," Dr. Fisher said, making a final notation on his clipboard and heading for the door. "It's not often we get a Jane Doe who's so —"

"J.D.," she said suddenly, turning the name over in her mind. Something about it sounded right.

"What?"

"That's what you can call me. J.D."

He tilted his head, as if listening hard to the sound of it, then nodded. "It suits you."

"I know."

"Okay, *J.D.* Everything's going to work out for you, I can feel it. They've found a nice place for you to stay, at least until all this confusion gets cleared up and you can go home. There are a lot of people looking out for you. Try not to be too scared."

"I'm not scared." And as she said it, she realized it was true. She was lost, she was alone, and she was even a little angry — at whoever had caused that explosion, at her parents, wherever and whoever they were. Even at herself. She just wasn't scared.

She had no memory of where she came from. She had no control over where she was going. Her mind couldn't be trusted, and two days ago she had almost died. She almost certainly *should* have been scared, but she wasn't. And maybe that was the scariest thing of all.

freak

"Watch it," the girl grunted, slamming her shoulder against J.D. as she pushed down the hall.

J.D. didn't say anything, just kept her head down and her shoulders hunched. She hadn't spoken a word since arriving at the Chester Center for Juvenile Services. The director had ushered her up the steps, past the flashing cameras and the thrusting microphones, and taken her directly to his office for a brief breakdown of life at the Center. When the lecture was over, he'd sent her directly to the dormitory, a long, narrow hall crammed with bunk beds. There was a lower bunk waiting for her, with a small blue footlocker next to it. The caseworker had given her three sweaters, a pair of jeans, a set of green pajamas, and clean underwear, and she put them all carefully inside. They were her only belongings — except for the clothes she'd been wearing when they found her. A pair of jeans, slightly too small for her and frayed at the bottom of each cuff. A white tee with a large yellow daisy stenciled on the front and rows of smaller daisies winding around the neck and hem. It was too young for her. Like the jeans, it was almost tight. And, like the jeans, it was ruined, covered in ash and grime from whatever had happened to her. Maybe, when she got up that morning three days ago, she had been missing her childhood and had slipped into an old outfit she'd outgrown long ago, just to remind herself of how things used to be. Or maybe *all* her clothes were too old and too small. Maybe, like the kids at the Center, that was all she'd been able to afford.

She stared at them. The clothes were her only link to her life *before*. They were her only clue to the past — and they weren't much of a clue at all.

As the other girls filed into the dorm room, J.D. had quickly stuffed the clothes into her locker and slammed the door shut. For some reason, she didn't want anyone else to see.

"Hey, it's the Girl without a Past!" the first girl to see her had crowed, bursting into braying laughter. The rest of her group joined in. J.D. ignored them.

She wouldn't be here for long — everyone had promised her that. She just needed to endure.

"Looks like the Girl without a Clue to me," another girl jeered.

That was the closest any of them came to talking to her.

They slammed into her in the halls, accidentally on purpose. On the way to the recreation room, a foot darted out in her path and she fell hard, catching herself just before her face slammed into the dirty linoleum. She cried out, more in surprise than in pain.

"No cameras to pose for here," a harsh voice said. J.D. looked up. A girl with close-cropped orange hair and an angry sneer loomed over her. She pointed down the hall, toward the doors that led to the outside world. "Out there, you may be a star. In here? You're no better than the rest of us. And no one cares what happens to you. So you'd better watch out."

Maybe you *should watch out*, J.D. thought defiantly, but something made her keep quiet. It didn't feel like fear. More like a cold voice in the back of her mind that said, *Wait. Not now, but soon.*

So she gritted her teeth and tried to ignore the

jeering crowd. She concentrated so hard on block-
ing them out, she almost didn't notice the hand
reaching down to help pull her up. But she grabbed
it and got back on her feet.

The boy, his shaggy dark hair hanging over his
eyes, snatched his hand away as soon as she was
upright. "Welcome to your worst nightmare," he mumbled, then turned away and started down the hall.

"Wait!" she called after him. "Thanks for —"

But he didn't stop, and soon she was alone again.

She saw him later in the cafeteria, sitting at
the end of a long metal table, hunched over his food.
He looked up as she came through the doorway, but
his eyes skimmed over her without pause or recog-
nition. She wasn't dumb enough to wave.

The cafeteria line moved slowly even though there
were no options. Everyone got the same scoop of
watery mashed potatoes and pile of limp green beans.
Everyone got a puddle of beef stew in the middle of
their plate and a stale cookie for dessert. But there
were a lot of mouths to feed, and no one was in
much of a hurry.

There were no empty tables, so J.D. chose the
emptiest she could find. She sat down at one end,

and everyone around her quickly picked up their trays and moved down to the other. As if she had a disease.

The chairs were bolted to the table, which was bolted to the floor. Everything was covered in a thin layer of dust and crumbs. She missed the hospital, where things had been clean and no one had hated her.

She wished she had something better to miss. She wished she remembered how to make friends.

But she didn't waste too much time on pointless wishing. Whoever she was, she wasn't that kind of girl.

"Look here, it's the Girl without a Spine." The orange-haired girl was back, with a pack of friends.

"Come on, Mel, can't we just go eat?" one of them complained softly.

Mel glared at her, then turned back to J.D. "I can't eat — she's making me sick."

"What's your problem?" J.D. said, trying not to stare at the long, thick scar that ran down Mel's cheek. It was the kind of scar you could only get in a fight, and J.D. wondered whether Mel had been on the winning or losing end.

"*You're* our problem," another of the lackeys said.

It was a guy with greasy black hair and a gold stud in his right ear. "Freak."

"I'm not a freak," J.D. said angrily.

"Don't even know who you are?" the guy retorted. "Sounds like a freak to me."

"Or maybe just a moron," a third girl said, laughing.

Mel's stare was cold. "Or maybe you *do* remember. Maybe you blew that place up yourself, and now you're just putting on an act, trying to get some attention."

J.D. rolled her eyes. "Right. And I almost blew myself up with it. Just for fun."

"That would make you a moron *and* a freak," the greasy-haired guy said eagerly. "Works for me."

"It would make you crazy," Mel said.

"Oh, is *that* your problem?" J.D. asked with fake wide-eyed innocence. "You're afraid I'm stealing your act? Don't worry, I'm sure I'm nowhere near as crazy as you."

With a sudden, smooth swoop of her arm, Mel knocked J.D.'s tray off the table. Clumps of mashed potatoes and stew went flying through the air, a chunk of soggy beef spattering against J.D.'s face before dropping to the floor. The clatter of the tray echoed loudly through the room, which had fallen completely silent. "Oops," Mel said coolly, jerking her head at her posse. Time to move on. "Just stay out of my way, freak."

J.D. stared back fiercely, wiping off the stew that smeared her cheek like a bloody gash. "Or what?"

Mel let the guy answer for her. "You don't want to find out," he said, rubbing his hands together in anticipation. "But you're gonna."

J.D. felt like the whole room was watching her. She waited for someone in charge to come over and punish Mel for destroying her lunch. But it didn't happen. There was a bored-looking guard standing by the exit who had seen the whole thing. But he didn't move. Eventually, a cafeteria worker came over to mop away the disgusting mess. But no one offered J.D. any more food.

She stared down at the table, a frozen smile fixed on her face. She could tell they were all looking at her, whispering about her, *laughing* at her. J.D. pretended not to care. Eventually, conversation shifted and the eyes turned away. People moved on with their lives — except J.D., who stayed frozen.

Until the scrawny boy, the one who'd helped her that morning, sat down beside her. "That wasn't very smart," he muttered without looking at her.

"What?"

"Talking back like that. You have to let it roll off your back. Only way you're going to survive." He slid his tray toward her. The stew was all gone, along with the beans, but there was still a full serving of mashed potatoes and a cookie. "Here."

She wasn't hungry anymore, but she gave him a small smile — a real one. "Thanks. I'm J.D."

He didn't say anything and for a moment, she thought he was going to leave as abruptly as he had before.

"Daniel," he said finally, still staring down at his food.

"Have you been here long?"

He just shrugged.

She tried again. "I guess you don't want to be here any more than I do."

His lips tightened into a thin line. Of course he didn't want to talk to her, she realized. He was a loser — but not as big a reject as she was. Being seen with her probably wouldn't do him any favors.

Or maybe he just wasn't a big talker.

30

Either way, she had already discovered that she wasn't the type who needed to babble nervously just to fill the silence. So she broke off a chunk of the cookie and nibbled on it, trying to ignore the slightly bitter undertaste. Daniel sipped from a carton of milk. When he'd finished it, he stood up, leaving her with the tray of food.

"Just keep your head down," he said in a soft voice. "You'll be fine."

You'll be fine. J.D. almost laughed. People kept saying that to her — and every time they did, things only got worse.

The Chester Center was for kids no one cared about — and because of that, it seemed that no one much cared what they did. During the week, there would be classes, but it was a Saturday, which meant there were only two options: look for trouble or watch TV.

J.D. dragged a metal folding chair over to the group of kids huddled in front of the screen. They were watching some stupid movie about a killer robot from the future, but J.D. didn't care. She was just glad they weren't watching the news.

Watching TV was the right idea. For the first time

since — well, as long as she could remember — she let herself relax. She barely paid attention to the movie, which seemed to be one long chase scene after another with a few explosions in between. Instead, she zoned out.

"Destroy it." The voice in her ear was a deep baritone, quiet but clear. J.D. whipped her head around, but no one was there. "Destroy it." The voice was louder now, insistent. J.D. was sure it was talking to her and though she didn't know what it was demanding, she felt compelled to obey. "Do it now."

No one else reacted. Either the movie was more engrossing than she'd thought — or the voice was only in her head.

J.D. felt a warm tingling in her fingers. It crawled up her arms like a horde of spiders and she opened her mouth —

Don't scream, she thought furiously. She was hearing a voice that no one else could hear. If anyone wanted proof that she was crazy, this would be all the evidence they needed. *Whatever you do, don't scream.*

Her arms and hands grew warmer and then a pulse of searing heat flashed through them, so intense she looked down, expecting them to be red and blistering. "Now!" the voice raged. A surge of anger shot through her. But it wasn't just anger, it was . . . *power.* She felt strong, like a current was rippling through her body, shooting out of her.

And then, an explosion.

She didn't just hear it, she *felt* it. A deafening boom, and everything began to shake. The world around her — the *real* world, she told herself, trying to hold on — faded, engulfed by the flames in her mind. She blinked, trying to focus on the people, the television, the walls — but they were nearly transparent. Superimposed over them was a green meadow and a wall of fire, crawling toward her. She blinked again. She could see the ceiling of the rec room — a moment later, all she saw was blue sky, thick with black smoke.

It's not real, she told herself, but she was choking on the foul stench of diesel fumes. Her eyes burned, and she shut them against the smoke. In the distance, she heard applause. Then the voice was back. She pressed her hands against her ears, but there was no shutting out the man inside her head. "Well done," he said, and she could almost feel his cold hand on her shoulder. "Well done."

"It wasn't me!" she cried. But the voice was finally silent.

When she dared to open her eyes again, the field was gone, along with the fire. There was nothing there but the rec room and the other kids. They had finally turned away from the TV screen.

They were all staring at her — and laughing.

J.D. tuned them out. She was too busy trying not to hyperventilate. *Your memories may return to you all at once, or they may come back in flashes*, Dr. Fisher had said.

A short, round woman in a cheap red blouse came over, and J.D. jerked away just before she could put a hand on her shoulder. She was afraid that if anyone touched her now, while she could almost still see the flames, she would have to scream. "Everything okay?" the counselor asked.

J.D. considered telling her the truth. But the woman didn't look like she wanted to hear it. And what was the truth? She didn't know what had just happened. Maybe it was a memory . . . except that she had seen the explosion site on the news, and it was in the center of a city, surrounded by cement. Just now, she had seen grass. And that wouldn't explain the voice.

What kind of memory comes to life like that, drowning out the real world? What kind of memory talks to you inside your head and makes you feel like your hands are on fire?

Maybe the kind of memory that's not a memory at all. The kind that's a hallucination. *If you start experiencing strange symptoms . . .*

"I'm fine," she mumbled. "I just need to . . . some air . . . uh . . . outside." She stood up and backed away from the group, stumbling over the leg of her chair and catching herself just before she fell. No one had turned back to the movie; instead, they were all watching her like she was some kind of car accident and they couldn't bear to turn away. Even the counselor.

J.D. felt a hot blush rising in her cheeks. She just needed to get out. Get *away*. Forcing herself not to run, she walked as quickly as she could toward the glass door at the back of the room. She pushed through it and raised her face to the sky, telling herself that the tears springing to her eyes were just a reaction to the cold, stinging wind.

There was a fenced-in area of blacktop just outside the rec room. A basketball court lay at one end, but no one was using it. Instead, the cement was covered by clumps of kids, some smoking, others just hanging out. None of them were looking in her direction, which was just what she needed.

J.D. longed for privacy, but she would settle for fresh air.

She took one deep breath, then another, letting the cold seep into her. She leaned back against the wall and closed her eyes. *This is real*, she told herself. *That was . . . something else.*

But nothing felt quite solid, and she half expected all this — the blacktop, the kids, the Center, every-thing — to disappear just as quickly as her vision had.

Vision, that was an okay word for it. Better, at least, than hallucination.

"Leave me alone!" Daniel's voice cried from the other side of the court. "Get off!"

"Shut up, crybaby!" Mel shouted, and the crowd cheered her on.

Maybe J.D. needed an escape from her own wor-ries; maybe she wanted to help the only person who had tried to help her. Maybe the anger, strength, and *power* she'd felt before were still coursing through her, bubbling just beneath the surface. She didn't stop to analyze, she just took off toward the sound of Daniel's voice.

A ring of kids had formed, with Daniel at the

center. Mel and her greasy-haired sidekick were pushing him back and forth, like they were playing catch. He was smaller than both of them and didn't have a chance. But his expression was fierce.

"Take it back, Kendall!" he yelled, as the greasy-haired boy swung his first punch. Daniel ducked out of the way and threw a weak punch of his own.

"You know it's true," Kendall taunted.

"I said *take it back*!" Daniel roared. He threw himself on Kendall. The bigger boy stumbled backward, but before Daniel could throw another punch, Mel grabbed his arms and pinned them behind his back.

"Little crybaby," she hissed. "Gonna cry for your mommy? She can't hear you, not where she is."

Daniel roared again, an incoherent jumble of pain and rage, cut short by Kendall's fist slamming into his nose.

J.D. didn't stop to think, wasn't capable of thought. A fog washed over her as she hurtled through the ring of kids, into the middle of the circle, and threw herself at Kendall. He pushed her away, and she stumbled back, almost falling. But she was still on her feet, and she rushed him again. Mel let go of Daniel and swung around toward J.D., grabbing her wrists hard and flinging her to the ground. J.D. crashed into the cement, her teeth slamming down on her tongue. The metallic taste of blood filled her mouth.

Mel was pulling something out of her pocket, something sharp that glinted in the sun. "Come and get me, freak," she taunted. But she didn't give J.D. a chance. Mel lunged for her, sweeping her arm down in a stabbing motion, and J.D. twisted out of the way just in time. She climbed to her feet, just as Mel came at her again.

Panic flooded over her, but there was a wall of kids behind her, trapping her in the circle. There would be no running away, no escape. Mel snarled and lunged again. J.D. thrust out her arms, knowing she couldn't stop Mel, couldn't stop a knife — and then someone screamed. It wasn't J.D.

Mel went flying backward through the air and landed in a heap several feet away, her head cracking against the concrete. She let out a moan and a small sigh — then was silent.

Everything froze.

J.D.'s heart thundered in her ears. Mel didn't move.

"I barely touched her," she whispered. But she wasn't sure. Her memories of the fight were already blurring. She had been defending herself, she knew that. There was no way she would have had the strength to throw Mel so far. Mel was so much bigger and stronger — and Mel was the one with the knife. She was the one who was ruthless.

Except that J.D. was still standing and Mel was lying on the ground with her face mashed into the concrete.

Kendall rushed to his friend's side. Daniel stared at J.D. *Everyone* stared at J.D.

"I didn't mean to," she protested, in a strangled voice. She told herself it was true. She had just wanted to protect Daniel, that was all. She had never meant to hurt anyone.

Right?

The kids were all backing away from her. But not the way they had in the cafeteria. They weren't ignoring her. They were backing away slowly, keeping a wary eye on her — like they were afraid of what she would do next.

She knew how they felt.

daniel

J.D. skipped dinner that night. No one noticed. While everyone else filed into the cafeteria, she stayed in the girls' dormitory, sitting on her bed, her knees curled up to her chest and her head grazing the iron springs of the upper bunk. She wanted to understand what had happened to her that afternoon, to sift through the events calmly and rationally and figure out what to do next. But it was hard to stay calm when she half expected that, at any moment, the deep voice would return, crawling in her ear, urging her to do terrible things. And there was no rational explanation for what had happened to Mel. What she'd *done* to Mel.

She worried she was going crazy — and she worried she wasn't. She'd already proven she was stronger than she'd thought; maybe she was tougher, too.

Maybe that's who she was, someone who liked to hurt people. Who knew how to — she shivered at the memory of the disembodied voice — *destroy*.

When lights-out came, J.D. pretended to be asleep. But she was wide awake with her eyes closed, and she could hear the whispers.

"Can you believe she didn't even get in trouble?" someone asked.

"Of course not, she's their special pet," another voice sneered. "Can't punish her with the cameras watching."

"She could've *killed* Mel. Did you see how far she threw her? I hear Mel has a broken collarbone."

"I guess Mel shouldn't have messed with her *boyfriend*."

"Where is Daniel, anyway? I figured he'd be sleeping in here tonight. Since now we all know he's such a *girl*."

They burst into nasty giggles. J.D. wanted to jump up and defend him again — not to mention defend herself. But that would only make things worse. And whatever reckless, blind energy had filled her that afternoon was gone. She was thinking again, and she thought it would be better to stay quiet.

One by one, the girls fell silent, but J.D. stayed awake. She was afraid the nightmares would come again and that, this time, she might actually remember what she had dreamed. The man might come back . . . or the fire. And when she woke up screaming, as she had every night in the hospital, the girls would know they'd been right. She was a freak.

But eventually, her eyes slid shut and she slipped down into the darkness. That night was a first.

She didn't dream at all.

At breakfast, J.D. sat down next to Daniel. He shot her a poisonous look, then stood up, lifted his tray, and walked away. He stood in the middle of the cafeteria for a moment, searching, and finally settled on a half-empty table across the room. As J.D. choked down her bowl of cold oatmeal, she watched Daniel nibble on the edge of a piece of toast. He didn't look around the first time someone threw a piece of bread at him. And he didn't react the second time, even when it bounced off his face and landed in his juice. Then Kendall walked past and dropped a dollop of oatmeal on his head.

Daniel stood up.

"What're you gonna do?" Kendall asked, hands resting on hips. His lip curled into a sneer. "You wanna fight me?"

Daniel's hands balled into fists.

"Or you just gonna get your freak girlfriend to protect you?"

"Shut up."

"Or what?" Kendall sneered. "I'm so scared. Are you gonna . . . *cry*?"

For one awful moment, it looked like Daniel might. Then he pushed Kendall out of the way and stormed toward the exit. He whispered something to the guard, who stepped aside. J.D. didn't hesitate. She followed him.

The guard pressed a meaty hand into her shoulder when she tried to pass.

"No one leaves," he grunted.

"That boy just left," she pointed out.

"Bathroom."

"That's where I'm going, too," she told him. He let her pass.

The corridor was empty; no one was allowed to be in the halls during mealtime. Daniel could have snuck back to his dormitory, but more likely, he had told the guard the truth and was hiding out in the guys' bathroom.

"Daniel!" she called, reaching the gray door with the cartoon stick figure painted on top.

"Go away!" he shouted back.

"Come out here," she said. "Please."

"Just stay away from me."

So he was stubborn? Fine. She could be stubborn, too. She had no identity, after all. She could be anything she wanted.

"Come out here, or I'm coming in," she called.

"Try it!"

The door was locked. She jiggled the handle. Definitely locked. But that was impossible. The doors in the Center locked — and unlocked — only with a key. "Let me in!" she shouted, her fists banging against the door with a satisfying *thump thump thump*. There was no answer. This was getting ridiculous. If someone caught her . . .

"If you don't let me in, someone's going to find me here!" she yelled, a smile crawling across her face. "And when they figure out you're the one inside . . ."

The door swung open. He didn't come out, so, as promised, she stepped in. Rolling his eyes, he closed the door behind her. Then he pulled something out of his pocket and turned his back on her so she couldn't see what he was doing to the knob. She heard a soft click. A moment later, he turned back around.

"This is the *boys'* bathroom," he pointed out.

"Whose fault is that?" J.D. retorted. "I tried to talk to you out there, but you weren't interested."

He turned away and retreated toward the sinks. "You know why."

Instead of answering, she took a long look around. It looked pretty much the same as the girls' room, except for the row of urinals lined up against one of the drab walls. And the faint smell of urine. The girls' room smelled a bit like the hospital, which meant it smelled so strongly of cleaning fluid that it almost burned the nose. But this place just smelled like a toilet.

"If you're here to apologize, don't bother."

"Apologize?" A laugh burbled out of her. "And I thought *I* was the crazy one. Why would I apologize to you?"

He whirled around to face her, fire in his eyes. "You made me look like a wimp yesterday," he said. "Like I needed a girl to protect me."

J.D. let out an exasperated sigh. "You *did* need a girl to protect you," she pointed out.

"I was doing fine before you got there."

"Kendall would have beat your brains in," J.D. argued.

"Like you did to Mel?"

Now she was the one who turned away. At least he wouldn't see her face go pale, and he couldn't guess that she felt like her throat was closing up.

"I hear she's going to be okay," he said quietly, almost gently, as if maybe he had guessed after all. He sighed. "Of course, as soon as she's back from the infirmary, she's probably going to try to kill you." Now his voice was rueful but casual, like he was talking about a baseball game about to be rained out. "And me, too."

"And I guess that's my fault?" she asked defiantly. "Is that what you want an apology for?"

"I don't want *anything* from you," he replied. "I never did."

"I was just trying to help."

"Who asked you to?"

"Who waits to be asked?" She took a step toward him, then another, until they were standing face-to-face, nose to nose, with only a foot of space between them. "So what now? Are you going to thank me, or do you want to try to beat me up or something, just to prove to everyone how tough you are?"

Daniel glared at her. "I could, you know."

"Just try it," J.D. warned him, and though she didn't want to fight him — or anyone — she was ready. Once again, she felt like she was watching herself, like she was watching a stranger. *Don't mess with her,* she thought. *She's tougher than she looks.*

"Maybe I will," he snapped.

"Fine."

"Fine."

She waited for him to make a move, wondering what she would do if he did. His eyebrows knit together in a dark cloud over his eyes, and his knees bent slightly, as if he was preparing to pounce. His hands clenched and unclenched, clenched and unclenched, warm-up exercises for his fists.

And then he burst into laughter.

It was the first time J.D. had ever seen him smile, and it was like seeing him for the first time. Without the perma-scowl, she could see his freckles, the dimple in his chin, and the funny way his ears jutted out from his head. He had a great smile, a little crooked, so that the left side stretched up higher than the right, revealing a small gap between his front teeth. It was the kind of smile that was catching, so she smiled back.

"You're . . . not the way I expected you to be," he said when he'd finally regained control of himself.

"Join the club."

"No, I just mean, there's something about you. You're not like the rest of us."

"I know," she snapped. "I'm the freak, remember?"

"No, not like that. Just . . . different."

"Different how?"

Daniel shrugged. "Different good." He held out a hand for her to shake. And though it was a weirdly formal gesture, especially considering they were standing on pee-stained linoleum in front of a row of urinals, it felt right. "I guess I *should* say thanks," he said.

She clasped his hand firmly. "And I guess I should say sorry."

He shook his head. "No. You shouldn't."

Daniel refused to talk about his own past, but he couldn't get enough of J.D.'s. All seventy-two hours of it.

"You really don't remember anything?" he asked again. "*Anything?*" They were sitting at a table in a back corner of the rec room, J.D. doodling in a notebook, Daniel twisting and untwisting a paper clip, winding it into an elaborate metal pretzel, smoothing it out into a straight line, then starting over again. At first, J.D. had been worried about what might happen when they were seen together, but Daniel knew better. "They may hate me," he'd said, "but they're *scared* of you."

"They hate me, too," she argued. "Especially after I didn't get in any trouble for . . . for what I did."

"True. But fear beats anger, every time."

And he was right; they weren't disturbed.

She shook her head. "Before a couple days ago, it's a total blank."

"But you must remember *something*," he pressed.

She shook her head again, trying not to think about the man's voice, the waking dream. *It wasn't a memory*, she told herself. It couldn't be. She didn't want to imagine what that would mean about her life — a life she might have to return to someday. *Destroy it*. The man's voice echoed in her head, and she shivered. *No,* she told herself firmly. It was just her imagination. The idea that the man could be real . . . it was just too terrifying. She would almost rather be crazy.

"The doctor said I'll remember eventually, especially if I'm around familiar stuff," she said, trying to sound unconcerned. "You know, people I know, places I've been, but . . ." She swept an arm out, to encompass their surroundings. He got the message.

"You won't be here for long," he told her.

"How do you know?"

"Because you belong to someone out there," he said. "Eventually your parents are going to find you, and they'll want you back."

"Unless . . ." She didn't want to say it out loud, the thing she'd been thinking. It had started out as a tiny worry, buried so deep in her mind that she could pretend it wasn't there. But with every hour that passed, it got bigger, more insistent. And speaking it aloud to someone, even Daniel, might make it real.

"Unless they don't want you, right?" he guessed. "Unless that's how you ended up out there on your own in the first place?"

Her muscles tightened, and she curled in on herself, folding her arms across her chest as if to protect herself from something. "If I belong to someone out there, why don't they come and get me?" she muttered, her head down. "Why would they just leave me here?"

Daniel's face was perfectly still, but a small muscle twitched in his jaw. "Good question."

Neither of them spoke for a long moment. J.D. concentrated on the page of doodles, which, she now realized, were all drawings of the same thing — a symbol:

Some of them were shaded in, some were simple, and some were elaborate. A few were outlined so heavily it looked like the pencil had almost broken through the page. A chill came over her, like someone was dripping ice water down her spine. She didn't know what the symbol meant. She hadn't realized what she was doing.

"So what are you drawing over there?" Daniel asked, leaning across the table to get a look. She slammed the notebook shut.

"Ooookay." He looked surprised but not offended. "You know what? Let's get out of here."

"And go where?" she asked skeptically. They were

in the middle of "free time," but there was nothing free about it. They were restricted to the rec room, the computer room, the library, and the blacktop. J.D. and Daniel had already hit the computer room — he hadn't been able to believe she didn't have an email address until she reminded him she didn't even have a name. The library was, according to Daniel, a dank space where the smaller kids read comic books and occasionally retreated to the dark stacks for a good cry.

The blacktop, for obvious reasons, was no longer an option.

"Trust me?" he asked, but he didn't wait around for an answer.

J.D. followed him out of the rec room. They took off down the hall toward the library, darting down a side corridor when the nearest guard had her back turned. Then it was down a stairwell and through a dark cavernous space, until they hit an imposing metal door. It was locked.

Daniel pulled out a small velvet case, about the size of a playing card, and selected two thin, silver-colored sticks. He stuck them into the lock, jiggled them back and forth and, a moment later, there was a click. He twisted the knob and swung the door open with a flourish. "*Voilà!*"

"How'd you . . . ?"

He held up the case. "Lock-pick kit. I got it last time they let us go into the city. Cost about ten bucks. Then I taught myself how to use it."

He flicked on a light switch and J.D. peered into the room they'd broken into. It looked like a storage area, stuffed with old furniture and musty cardboard boxes. She pressed her hand to her mouth, trying to hold back a sneeze. It didn't work.

J.D. couldn't help but wonder why Daniel had dragged her down here. It was kind of depressing, a room of stuff so unwanted that even the rejects upstairs had rejected it. Maybe he wanted to explore or raid it for treasure. She would have preferred to stay in the doorway, playing with the lock-pick kit. She liked the way the silver glinted in the light — and liked the idea of being able to escape.

J.D. rubbed her wrist, remembering the soft, fluffy grip of the leather cuffs, and how it had felt to be chained in place.

"What are we doing here?" she asked, trying, for once, to push away a memory.

Daniel extended a closed fist, then opened his hand, palm side up, to reveal one of the slender silver picks. "Thought you might want to learn how." He looked around, then gave her another of his rare but brilliant smiles. "This is a good spot. No one to bother us."

He showed her how to slip in the tension wrench, a long, narrow tool slightly thicker than the picks, and twist it, like she was turning a key. Then slide the pick in, feeling for the pins that held the lock in place, listening for the soft, telltale click, then moving on to the next one. He taught her about the different kind of locks, pin-and-tumbler, wafer tumbler, tubular, reciting the terms softly and reverently, like just saying the right name would be enough to open a door. He talked about the moment just before the lock turned, when you knew you had it, when you could feel everything falling into place. It was a certainty deep down, he explained, knowing that you were about to break through.

Then he let her go solo, and she experienced it for herself.

When she had finally mastered the mechanism and could pick the lock in under ten seconds, he declared her first lesson a success. Then he leaned against the wall and let himself slide down to the floor, stretching his legs out and propping his arms behind his head. She realized he didn't want to go back upstairs any more than she did.

J.D. dropped down beside him. Daniel kept up a low but steady monologue, like he knew that she wasn't in the mood to talk. He told her about the other kids — how Mel had been bounced out of four foster homes and always ended up back at the Center, how Kendall sometimes woke up crying. He talked about the work placement program he would be eligible for as soon as he turned fifteen — in just a few weeks — and how, if he was lucky, he could find a place where he could work *and* live, far away from the Center. He talked about what he would do, someday, when he was eighteen and could escape the system for good.

He said nothing about where he'd been before he got to the Center, except that it had been much worse.

"Sometimes forgetting the past's not so bad," he told her. "Sometimes it's worse to remember."

It happened without warning.

J.D. was relaxed, close to happy, almost hopeful that she could learn to deal. She had spent the day with

Daniel. She had a *friend*. And now she was back in the cafeteria, and he was by her side, and it didn't matter who saw them together. It was like an invisible force field protected them from everything, and if kids were staring or laughing or throwing things, they didn't have to notice it if they didn't want to. It didn't matter that the dinner was disgusting — another stew, with greenish-yellow things floating in it that might have been vegetables. It almost didn't matter that this was her second night here — the fifth night of her new life — and no one had come to claim her.

Daniel was sitting across from her, telling her some story about his homeroom teacher's spider phobia, and she was laughing, not because Daniel's impression of the man's face after the spider landed on his bald spot was particularly funny, but because it felt good to laugh. And then she heard it.

It began quietly, nearly drowned out by her laughter and Daniel's voice. Then it grew louder, more insistent. The lilting melody danced up and down, the notes bleeding into each other. "What *is* that?" she asked, breaking into his story.

"What?"

But she didn't need the look of confusion on his face to tell her that the music was in her head. It was the same melody she'd heard in the hospital. She started to say, "Nothing — just thought I heard something" when the music swelled and she stopped.

Stopped speaking, stopped moving, stopped thinking.

It was like everything froze. And then, as if the music was speaking to her — or *through* her — she knew what she had to do.

She picked up the glass juice bottle from the edge of her tray, stared at it, imagined how good it would feel to smash it in her fingers, the glass shattering, slicing, scattering to the ground. And with the barest squeeze of her fingers, it did.

Shatter. Explode into a million shards. Purple juice gushed everywhere, drenching her hands. She ignored it.

"Are you okay?"

The voice was distant, unimportant.

"J.D.? What are you doing? J.D.!"

She ignored it.

Amid the glittering pieces of glass, she spotted a long shard, its edges sharp. It called to her, and she picked it up, ignoring the thin trickle of red that ran down her palm. She felt no pain. Only determination.

The boy. He was shouting, waving, turning colors. No matter. She gripped the shard tighter, pictured the jagged red line she would scrape across his skin.

She raised the shard of glass over her head, ready to bear down, preparing to strike. The boy lunged toward her, catching her wrist as it sliced downward, wrenching it hard enough to knock the piece of glass out of her hand. She pushed him back, but he'd twisted her off balance and her feet tangled in the legs of the chair and she tipped backward —

The music stopped.

She didn't know why she was on the floor. She didn't know why her hand was bleeding or why Daniel was standing over her, a mix of fear and concern on his face.

"J.D.?" He hesitated for a moment, then reached out a hand to help her up, just like he had the first time she saw him. "Are you . . . okay?"

"What happened?" she asked. Her hand was throbbing. Daniel waved off the guard, who had rushed over, mumbling something about an accident. There was broken glass everywhere.

"You don't remember?" He looked alarmed. "The bottle, it just broke in your hand, then you had that piece of glass, and I was afraid you were going to hurt yourself or something, and . . . You really don't remember?"

She saw it in flashes, the breaking glass, the blood, the struggle. She remembered the need to hurt someone. *Daniel?* It was like an echo, distant but still real. Like the music, which was gone, but left a trace of itself, like a ghost in her mind. The memories fought their way to the surface and she knew that if she let them, if she wanted to know, they would bubble up to the top. Whatever it was she'd done — almost done — would be a part of her.

She pushed it down, away. Buried it all.

So that when she shook her head and said, "No, I don't remember any of it," she was telling the truth.

promise

The field is a deep, fertile green, spotted with freckles of baby blue. She stoops, plucks a tiny blue flower from the long grass, brushes it against her chin. She breathes deep, sucking in the air, which has weight and tastes fruity and fresh, like a slice of apple.

Her hands tingle, a prickly pins-and-needles burn that spreads up her arms, up her neck, down her back, covers her with warm certainty. A shadow falls across the meadow, a round, black sinkhole in an ocean of bright green. She looks up. Closes her eyes. Raises her hands.

There is a sharp whistling noise, then a crack.

The ground shakes when the wounded helicopter falls out of the sky. Flames sprout, eating the grass and the flowers. Shouts in the distance, and the fire burns bluish-green, shooting up sparks. Metal screams, plastic melts, everything burns. She can feel the heat baking her face. Smell the poisonous smoke that makes her choke. She bends at the waist,

*coughing, spitting. A hand rubs slow circles against her
back.*

"You did it," he says. Not accusing. Proud.

*She turns and squints in the sun. His face is dark, in
shadow, unknowable. "You did it," he says again.*

And just before he turns away . . .

She sees his face . . .

J.D. popped up in bed, whacking her forehead
against the metal springs of the upper bunk. The
sharp pain dragged her back to waking life. But she
could still see the man's face in her head: cruel, thin
lips; bushy gray eyebrows that matched the thin-
ning, fraying strands combed across his forehead;
high cheekbones; and a nose, sharp and oversized,
that commanded attention. She knew him.

She knew his voice.

Just a dream, she told herself, trying to stop shaking. She didn't want it to be real.

She told herself she was just upset over what had
happened at dinner. She told herself that the dreams
were not memories. That soon she would remember
the truth about her past, and then the nightmares
would stop.

It was the kind of cool reasoning that worked

when the lights were on. But huddled in the dark, listening to the creaks and scuffling of the old building, catching flickering and fluttering motions at the corners of her eyes, figures in the shadows, it had no effect.

J.D. lay down again, turning her pillow over to the side that wasn't wet with tears. She was afraid to close her eyes, but leaving them open was almost worse.

"You did it." The man's voice echoed in her head.

She imagined she could still smell the acrid smoke. The palm of her hand throbbed, and she ran her fingers over the bandage, wincing at the pressure. She couldn't stand it, lying there, listening to the other girls breathe, waiting for something terrible to happen. And sleep might be the most terrible thing of all.

Disgusted by her fear — of shadows and dreams and her own mind, of *nothing* — she sat up again, ducking under the metal bar. The room was asleep, and there was no one to stop her from climbing out of bed and padding barefoot to the door, then down the empty hall toward the boys' dorm. She needed to see Daniel. She didn't know what help he could be, or what she would do next. She just knew she couldn't survive another night of feeling so alone.

The door had a large window in it. She stood on her toes, her nose pressed against the glass. The bunks were lined up against the walls, just like the girls' dorm. It was impossible to tell which one held Daniel — from this distance, they all looked the same. But he had told her he slept in the farthest corner, among the younger kids, who sometimes woke him when they had a particularly bad dream.

This was a bad idea, she decided.

Then footsteps came clomping down the hall, and she had no choice but to swing open the door and swiftly, silently slip inside.

She held her breath and stayed on her tiptoes, afraid that the slightest sound would give her away. If one of the boys woke up and discovered her trespassing . . .

Daniel slept on his side, his head hunched and his knees curled up toward his chest. His pajamas, supplied by the state, were the same dull green as hers. The thin blanket had been kicked to the foot of the bed, unnecessary when the boiler was running full blast, trapping the Center in a dry, blistering summer that never ended. He was whispering something in his sleep. J.D. couldn't hear the words and didn't want to. It felt like a violation.

She touched him lightly on the shoulder, then jumped back as he swung his arms out wildly, as if to ward off an attack. He opened his eyes.

"I couldn't sleep," she admitted in a whisper, giving him a half smile.

"Then what are we waiting for?" He straightened up and swung his legs over the side of the bed. "Let's go."

The chapel was no longer used on a daily basis or on much of a basis at all. A thick layer of dust lay over everything — the cracked wooden pews, the dingy red carpet, the low altar with its non-denominational messages of love and peace. J.D. paused for a moment in the aisle, sensing that she was supposed to feel some sense of awe or wonder, but feeling nothing. Then Daniel tugged at her arm and led her to their destination, a small alcove off to the side, even more forgotten than the chapel itself.

The dust was so thick that she could see it swimming through the tracks of moonlight that filtered through the windows. The back wall was lined with chairs and desks, stacked to the ceiling. Overstuffed plastic bags were clustered by the door. A third wall was dominated by a massive, arch-shaped stained-glass window with a central panel of clear glass that almost perfectly framed the moon.

Daniel stood in front of the window, arms linked behind his back, staring up at the glass panels. Some were too dim to make out, but in some the moon lit up the figures — a lion roaring, a bird, a boy stretching toward the sky, and a woman clutching something in her arms. J.D. thought it might have been a baby.

"I come here sometimes. It's quiet," he said without turning his head. "You want to talk about it?"

"Not really."

"Okay."

She was grateful he didn't push her to explain anything. She wasn't ready to talk. And it was easy to be quiet here — not just outside, but inside. Somehow, in this place, she was able to quiet the voices in her head. She was able to unclench her mind, stop straining for answers, and just float along on the ebb and flow of her thoughts.

Maybe this was the moment, then, that her memories would come rushing back, and she would learn who she really was.

But time passed, and she was still as much of a stranger to herself as ever.

She stared out at the sky and wondered. What had it been like, her life? Had she ever stood frozen and silent, staring up at the moon? Had she snuck out of the house to meet a friend — not because she was terrified of being alone, but because she was bored or it would be fun?

Had she *ever* had fun?

J.D. closed her eyes, trying to imagine a life for herself. She tried to picture a mother and a father, a warm house, looking up at the sky through a bedroom window, surrounded by familiar things. She tried to imagine knowing herself.

But her imagination, so overactive that afternoon, failed her now. And her mind stayed blank.

Enough time passed that the moon moved. The light shifted, and Daniel, who was standing a few steps behind her, sucked in a sudden, sharp breath.

"What is that?" he asked. "On your neck?"

"What?" She reached a hand back and touched her skin, but there was nothing there.

"It's, it's like, I think it's a . . ." He shook his head. "Your hair's kind of covering it. Can I . . . ?"

She nodded and bent her head as he parted the stray strands of hair. His fingers were cold on the nape of her neck. "It's a tattoo," he said finally. "Who gets a tattoo on the back of their neck?"

"Someone like me, I guess." She pressed her hand against her neck, imagining a long needle digging into it, injecting its shot of ink, then sliding out and stabbing her again and again, like a sewing needle, branding her with a permanent mark. She wondered: How much had it hurt? When did she get it — and why? "What's it a picture of?"

"It's some kind of symbol. Sort of — wait." He turned away from the stained glass and went over to the adjacent wall, where a row of low windows was covered in a sheen of dust. Daniel slid his right index finger against the dust, made a few quick swoops, then stepped back in satisfaction. "It's like that," he said. "Anything familiar?"

The symbol stood in sharp relief against the thick coating of dust, the moon lighting it with a pale glow:

"Yes." Her mouth formed the word, but no sound

came out. The same symbol covered the pages of her notebook. She'd drawn it herself, over and over again. But what did it — what did *any* of it — mean?

"J.D.?" There was a torn piece of cardboard lying on the sill, and he picked it up and began playing with it, bending it back and forth, then tearing off tiny brown strips. "What's up?"

She couldn't do this anymore. She couldn't just wander blindly, waiting for something to make sense, waiting for the uncertainty to fall away. She couldn't stand feeling helpless and confused and afraid. For all she knew, she would feel that way forever, unless she did something to stop it. Took action. Started figuring things out.

But she didn't want to do it alone.

"There's some stuff I should probably tell you," she began, wondering if Daniel would still be there when she finished. "For one thing, I've been having these dreams — and, uh, not just when I'm asleep."

She told him everything — the nightmares, the music, the symbols, the voice in her head, her visions of explosions, and the strange certainty that she had caused them. When she was done and it was all out, she expected to feel better — lighter. But the opposite happened. Saying it all at once like that made her realize that, whatever she wanted to tell herself, something was very wrong. This couldn't be normal.

She couldn't be normal.

While she was speaking, she had looked away. Now she watched Daniel's face closely for some clue to his reaction. His expression revealed nothing. His mouth was frozen in a deep frown, and his eyes never left hers. He didn't speak. She waited, her heart racing. If he was going to walk away, if he was going to label her a freak and leave her all alone again, she just wanted to get it over with.

"So, what do we do next?" he finally said.

"We?"

"We should find out more about the explosion, I think, and see if we can come up with any clues about what you were doing there, and then maybe —"

"Daniel."

"There must have been a bunch of newspaper reports and photographs. We can find them all online," he pressed on, getting lost in the plan. "And maybe we can find out something about memory loss. This doctor doesn't sound like he knew what he was talking about —"

"Daniel!"

"What?"

"You don't think . . ." She tried to shrug, like it was no big deal. "You know, that I'm crazy? That I should just go back to the hospital, and . . ."

"You're not crazy," he said flatly. "I've seen crazy. This is . . . something else. Maybe your memory's coming back."

J.D. froze. The thought that the field, the fire, the *man* might all be real didn't give her too much comfort. "I don't know."

"You just need to find out who you are and where you came from," Daniel insisted. "You need to find your way home. And we can do that."

What if we can't? she wanted to ask, but didn't, because he sounded so tough and sure, and she wanted to be, too.

"Why would you help me?" she asked instead. "You barely know me."

"I know you better than anyone else," he pointed out.

She almost smiled. "That's not saying much."

"It's enough for me. Besides . . ." He rubbed his left temple, where a black eye from the day before was blooming into a deep flower of purple, red, and blue. "I owe you one."

70

Bad enough she hadn't been punished for what she'd done to Mel; she didn't want to be rewarded for it. "You don't have to . . ."

"It's not because of that," he said quickly. "We're in this together now."

"Whatever *this* turns out to be?"

"Whatever. We can handle it." He gestured toward the door. "Tonight we sleep. Tomorrow, we figure this thing out."

J.D. felt tears sprouting at the edges of her eyes and blinked furiously to hold them back.

"Uh, you're not going to cry now, are you?" he asked, sounding half worried and half disgusted.

"Of course not."

"Because you can, if, you know . . ."

She gave him a light shove. "Are *you* going to cry?"

"Of course not!"

"Then we're even." She ducked through the door first so he wouldn't see her expression. Her voice held steady, and she knew she sounded determined. "Tomorrow we get some answers." And as they crept back through the dark hallway together, she felt lighter, no longer afraid of what the answers might be — or that she might never find them.

Morning meant possibility and the hope for change. She wasn't afraid of what it would bring. But getting to morning meant making it through the rest of the night . . . and she was still afraid to sleep.

wanted

There were no more dreams. Although she'd gotten only a few hours of sleep, she woke up just after dawn feeling refreshed. Today was the day for answers.

But as the girls filed out for breakfast, the monitor caught J.D. by the shoulder and pulled her aside. "You're to go to the administration office," she said.

J.D. drew a sharp breath. Someone must have found out that she'd snuck out of the dorm the night before. Maybe one of the other girls had noticed her empty bed and ratted her out. Would they punish her for that, when they had barely even yelled at her for what had happened to Mel? (*What I did to Mel*, she corrected herself.)

"Hurry up," the woman said brusquely.

J.D. didn't hurry, but it wasn't a long walk and she

found herself in front of the imposing office door sooner than she would have liked. The secretary looked up and gave her a wink. "Head on in."

The door to the administrator's office was thicker than the other doors in the Center. Its shiny white veneer looked out of place against the dingy wood frame, as if the original door had crumbled away and all hopes were pinned on this modern replacement to hold back the hordes. She glanced down at the knob and wondered if Daniel had ever tried to pick the lock.

"Go on, Jane," the secretary encouraged her. "They're waiting for you."

J.D. didn't bother to correct her on the name.

The door stuck at first, then popped open to reveal the head of the Center, Mr. Hopewell, sitting behind his cheap aluminum desk. The office was no more opulent than the rest of the building. When J.D. had sat there three days before, her gaze wandering while Mr. Hopewell laid out the rules and regulations, she'd fixed on the faded brown splotch in one corner of the ceiling. It seemed to have gotten twice as big since her last visit.

She didn't notice the woman at first. By the time she did, it was too late. "Alexa!" the stranger shrieked, darting out of the corner, rushing across the room, and throwing her arms around J.D. "Thank god!" Her voice was muffled, pressed into the top of J.D.'s head. J.D. breathed in the strong scent of lavender and endured the embrace, her arms stiff at her sides.

The woman didn't let her go but grabbed her by the shoulders, holding her out and squeezing tight enough that J.D. couldn't squirm away. "Honey, don't you remember me? I thought . . ." Her voice broke, and she looked helplessly at Mr. Hopewell, then back at J.D. "They told me, but I thought maybe once you saw me . . ." She stared down at J.D., peering into her eyes as if trying to pass along a silent message, then finally let go. The broken look on her face disappeared, and when she spoke again, her tone was calm.

"Your name is Alexa Collins," she said. "And I'm your mother."

J.D. waited to feel something — a jolt of familiarity, a flood of affection, a rush of relief. But there was nothing. This woman was a stranger.

"It's true," Mr. Hopewell said, a wide smile on his face. "This is your mother, Alexa. She's come to take you home."

"I don't know you," J.D. said, not caring that she

sounded cold. She turned to Mr. Hopewell, like there was something he could do. "I don't know her."

The woman lifted a hand to touch her again, but she jerked away. "Alexa . . ."

"That's not my name!"

"Yes. It is." Her voice softened. "I know you've been through a lot, hon —"

"And where were *you*?"

"Looking for you," the woman — her mother — said. She tapped a finger against her lips. "I was going out of my mind. I can't imagine how you ended up so far away, and now that I've found you . . ."

"If you're my *mother* . . ." Her mouth twisted on the word. J.D. didn't understand why she wasn't feeling happier. Maybe because she'd thought that if she could just find out who she was and where she belonged, it would change everything. But nothing had changed, except that this woman was claiming her. And she had another name that didn't fit. *Alexa Collins.* Another stranger. "Where's my father?"

The woman flinched, almost imperceptibly, like she'd been steeling herself for the question but it had hit harder than expected. "He passed away," she said softly. "Seven years ago. It's just the two of us now."

She gave J.D. a hopeful smile. "That's what we always say, the two of us against the world."

Without thinking, J.D. smiled back.

"Why don't you go get your stuff, Alexa?" Mr. Hopewell said. "I've got some things to discuss with your mother before you go, and I assume she'll want to check in with our staff doctor to go over all the medical files —"

"We have a family doctor who will be more than up to the task," the woman cut in. "If you just pass along the reports, that'll be adequate."

Mr. Hopewell opened and shut his mouth a couple times without saying anything and shuffled the stack of papers on his desk. "Fine. Fine, then. Just a few forms to sign, and we'll have you two on your way."

"*Now?*" J.D. asked, feeling a sudden tinge of panic. Not that she'd enjoyed life at the Center, but at least it was a known quantity. And Daniel was here. They were supposed to start figuring things out.

It finally occurred to her that she didn't need to search for answers anymore. They were all here in front of her — her name, her past, her mother. The woman was several inches taller than J.D. but just as thin. The blue cuffs on her tailored gray jacket perfectly matched her silk blouse and the thin blue lining around the bottom of her gray skirt. She had long, straight, straw-colored hair pulled neatly into a black barrette at the nape of her neck. Behind the wire-rim glasses, her eyes were the color of a tropical sea, a blue-green so bright they almost glowed.

She looks like me, J.D. thought in wonder, and for the first time, began to consider what it might mean that she had a mother. That this was her.

"Where will you take me?" she asked.

Her mother smiled and put her hand on the small of J.D.'s back. This time, J.D. didn't twist away. "Home," she said. "Where else?"

Her mother wanted to leave immediately, but J.D. — she just couldn't think of herself as Alexa, not yet — insisted on returning to the dorm and collecting her belongings. She went alone.

There wasn't much, but it was all she had, a record of the five days that made up the only life she knew.

"You have everything you need at home," her mother had said. "Just leave all that junk behind."

But J.D. couldn't. She took out the green pajamas and the handful of used clothing from the footlocker, folding each item neatly and putting it into a plastic bag. Then came the clothes she'd been wearing when they found her. J.D. stared at the shirt, the jeans, the blue sneakers with the gray stripes along each side, wondering what the girl wearing them had been thinking — wondering what had happened to her and where she had gone. It suddenly occurred to J.D. that she didn't need to wonder anymore. She could just ask her mother. It also occurred to her that now, the outfit didn't much matter — the clothes weren't her only link to her past. They were just clothes. She probably had a whole closet full of them.

At home.

She took one last look around, and was almost ready to go, when she spotted the envelope sitting on her pillow. Her name — J.D. — was written on the front in block letters.

J.D.,
I heard about your mom. Awesome. Wish I could get out of here, too. Guess you got your answers, right? But just in case:
dannyboy16@worldmail.net
So you know where to find me. If you need me. They wouldn't let me skip class to say good-bye, but I left you something. Maybe you'll need it, but I hope you don't. I know you're

going to remember everything, soon. Just don't forget me.

D

She bit her lip sharply to keep the tears welling in her eyes from falling. Then she read on.

PS. This time I made you cry, didn't I? You're such a girl!

And as a tear spattered down on the page, she laughed.

J.D. pulled Daniel's gift out of the envelope. It was the thin, silver tension wrench and a lock pick. Just in case she needed it, though he hoped she didn't. She put the letter back in the envelope and placed it carefully in her bag, on top of her clothes. She was about to do the same with the wrench and pick but then stuffed them into her pocket instead. It seemed safer to keep them close.

She had slept here for only two nights. It wasn't *her* bed any more than the one she'd left behind at the hospital. And there was no reason to feel sad, she told herself. She was going home.

Flashbulbs popped.

"Alexa! How did it feel to see your mother's face?"

"Are you happy to be going home?"

"Have you remembered anything about your past?"

"What were you doing in the warehouse district? Can you remember the explosion?"

"Alexa! Alexa! Over here!"

"Just a few questions, Alexa!"

The moment J.D. stepped out of the Center, the reporters surged forward, throwing out questions and pressing against her, until all she could see was a mass of cameras and microphones shoved in her face. J.D. tucked her head down and tried to barrel through.

She thought about the other kids who had walked through that door and down those steps with some stranger by their side, abandoned kids heading out for a new life. She doubted any reporters had chased after them.

Her mother's hand pressed down on her shoulder. "It's okay to talk to them, if you want."

It was the opposite of what J.D. wanted. How could her own mother not realize that? Had Alexa Collins loved the spotlight?

J.D. realized that she was thinking about herself in the third person . . . and the past tense. But Alexa wasn't gone. *Alexa is me*, she thought, trying out the sound of it in her mind. It sounded wrong. But maybe that didn't matter; maybe she should give it a try.

"I feel really lucky," she finally said, forcing herself to smile into a camera lens. She would tell them what they wanted to hear and maybe they would just go away. "I can't wait to get away from" — *all of you*, she thought — "all this and back to normal." She glanced up at her mother, who wore a proud smile. This was, apparently, the daughter she wanted — happy, well-behaved, and eager to return to her old life. J.D. wondered how long she could keep up the act. Maybe Alexa would return soon, and J.D. wouldn't have to fake it. She knew she should look forward to reclaiming her memories and her past, and until now, she'd wanted nothing else. But it suddenly occurred to her: When Alexa came back, what would happen to J.D.?

home

They arrived at the house an hour later.

"Does anything look familiar?" her mother asked anxiously, steering the black sedan into the driveway.

J.D. stared at the small two-story house in front of them. It had white siding, two windows on the upper floor and one large one at ground level, a single-car garage, a narrow lawn, and a winding path leading from the sidewalk to the front door. Her house sat at the end of a block lined with identical structures — every home in the neighborhood looked exactly the same. J.D. knew she should have memories of bike-riding on the sidewalk and trick-or-treating at the neighbors' houses and building snowmen on the lawn. The neighborhood looked quiet and family-friendly, and perfect for people who didn't want to worry about whether they were better or worse off than their neighbors. A tricycle lay on its side in one of the front yards, and several of the driveways had basketball hoops. It looked like it would have been a nice place to grow up.

"Nothing," she told her mother. "It's like I've never been here before. How long have you — we — lived here?"

"Your whole life," her mother said. She reached out an arm toward J.D., but then appeared to think better of it. Instead, she made a grab for the plastic bag. "Let me take this for you."

Without thinking, J.D. snatched it back. "I have it," she snapped. Then, instantly feeling a stab of guilt, she forced a smile. "I just mean, I can carry it."

"I thought maybe you'd want to bake some brownies," her mother suggested, as they stepped inside. "You've always loved brownies. And then for dinner, I'm making all your favorites, and . . ."

"I'm actually kind of tired," J.D. interrupted. "Can I, uh, go up to my room for a while?"

"Of course. I shouldn't have — yes. You're home now, this is your house, too, you can do whatever you want. I can call you when dinner's ready, if you'd like."

"Okay." J.D. didn't move. She stood in the

hallway, her shoes muddying the beige tile and her hands clutching her plastic bag to her chest. She waited. Then, finally, in a small voice, "Uh . . . where do I go?"

She hadn't known it was possible for a face to change so much without moving at all. But somehow, even though her mother's smile remained fixed in place, everything about her radiated sadness. Maybe it was the tight lines at the corners of her mouth or the way, for a long moment, she didn't move at all, didn't even blink. Or maybe it was just her eyes. Then she laughed softly, and the laughter had a cruel undertone, as if she was scolding herself. "Of course you don't know where to go," she murmured. "Up the stairs, second door on your left. That's your room. Everything's just the way you left it when . . ."

J.D. nodded and started up the stairs, which were covered by a shaggy brown carpet. At least she wouldn't leave any more footprints. She froze midway up when her mother called out.

"Alexa —" Catching the look on J.D.'s face, she winced apologetically. "Honey, I just wanted to say . . . I'm glad you're back. And safe. I love you."

J.D. would have given anything to be able to say "I love you" back and mean it, but her throat had closed up so tightly that she couldn't say anything. So she just nodded again, knowing it wasn't good enough, and continued up the stairs.

"How is it?" her mother asked anxiously. "Is there too much cheese? Do you want more sauce?"

"It's fine," J.D. told her — for the fourth time. She broke off another tiny piece of the baked ziti and brought the fork to her mouth, trying to gulp it down. Not that it tasted *bad*, exactly — it was certainly better than anything she'd had at the hospital or the Center — she just didn't like it. At least not the way she was supposed to.

J.D. took a swig of the chocolate milk, apparently her "favorite," even though it was way too sweet. The glass left a ring of milk on the white table, and she quickly wiped it off with a napkin, hoping her mother hadn't noticed. There were no stains and no dust anywhere in the house, no spots on anything except the muddy tile in the entry hall. J.D. had already deduced that her mother must be a neat freak. The big kitchen was white and spotless, except for the red splatter on the floor where J.D. had accidentally splashed some of her tomato sauce. It didn't look like the kind of place where people actually lived, and she didn't know how *she* was supposed to live there without ruining everything.

"Alexa, I want to take you to see someone tomorrow," her mother said suddenly. "A family friend. Dr. Styron."

J.D. tensed. "Dr. Fisher said I wouldn't need a checkup for another week, and I wanted to go back to him."

"Dr. Styron isn't — he's not that kind of doctor, honey."

"I don't get it."

Her mother drummed the fingers of her left hand against the table, and J.D. noticed that the nails were perfectly trimmed and covered in a soft pink polish. She wasn't wearing a wedding ring.

"He's a psychiatrist," she admitted. "He's known you since you were a baby, and he has some ideas for how to help you."

J.D. stared down at her plate. "Dr. Fisher said I would remember on my own," she mumbled.

"Some ER doc at a city hospital, what does he

know?" her mother snapped, her lips curling into a sneer that disappeared as soon as it had formed. She rubbed her hand across her eyes. "I just think it would be good to get a second opinion. Alexa, honey, don't you *want* to remember?"

"Yeah." J.D. sighed. "Of course I do."

"So shouldn't we do everything we can to make that happen?"

J.D. shrugged. It's not that she didn't want to remember — she was *desperate* to remember. But another doctor? More treatment? More people trying — and maybe failing — to fix her? She was tired of feeling like a patient, a poor victim who needed healing. She was finally home — safe — and she just wanted to learn how to be Alexa again. How to be normal.

Her mother leaned back in her chair. "I'm not going to force you, Alexa. But will you at least think about it?"

"Okay." J.D. looked away, not wanting to see whatever was in her mother's eyes, and focused on the clean white surface of the kitchen table instead.

Her mother's plate was almost clean. J.D.'s was still mostly full.

"When you were little, you loved noodles more than anything else," her mother said, smiling at the memory. "But you would only eat them with ketchup."

"Ketchup?" J.D. repeated, trying to picture herself as a little kid.

"Nothing but ketchup, on everything." Her mother laughed. "One day when you were coloring, I went upstairs to answer the phone, and when I came back, I found you sitting in front of a huge pile of ketchup. You were dipping your crayons in it, and when I asked you what you were doing, you said, 'They didn't taste good.' Then you popped one in your mouth and said, 'Now they do.'"

"No way." J.D. started giggling.

Her mother nodded. "When I took the crayons away, you started screaming so loud I was afraid the neighbors were going to call the police. But then I gave you some carrot sticks, and, with the ketchup on them, you didn't seem to know the difference."

"I ate carrot sticks dipped in *ketchup*?"

"Well, you *were* only three years old at the time."

J.D. took another bite of the baked ziti. It was starting to taste a little better. "Sounds like I was kind of a brat."

"Sometimes." Her mother laughed again, louder this time. "Especially when you were a baby. You could cry for hours. It was horrible, your little face would turn red and you'd just let out these ear-piercing screams and no one could get you to stop, except . . ."

"Except what?"

"You always stopped crying as soon as your father picked you up," her mother said softly. "He would pick you up and cradle you against his chest, and you would just smile. . . ." She pressed a hand over her eyes and took a long, shuddery breath. "Excuse me," she said in a high, thin voice and abruptly left the room.

J.D. found her in the study, bent over in a red leather chair, her shoulders shaking. "I'm sorry," she said, sensing J.D.'s presence without looking up. She took several deep breaths. J.D. wanted to do something, anything, but instead just stood there, helpless. "I know you don't remember me. I can deal with that. We'll figure it out. But the fact that you don't remember your father . . ." J.D.'s mom sat up, revealing a face streaked with tears. Her glasses were on her desk, and without them, she looked younger — and weaker. "He loved you so much," she whispered, blotting her nose with a tissue. "You need to know that. He was a wonderful man, and he just . . ." The tears began to flow again, and she covered her face. "I've never let you see me cry before. Even when — it happened, you never . . ."

J.D. reached out a hand and patted her mother's shoulder lightly. "I'm sorry," she said, surprised to feel tears springing to her own eyes. "I wish I could remember, I really do."

Her mother clutched J.D.'s hands in hers and squeezed them. "Thank you for saying that." She smiled weakly. "We'll get through this. We always do."

J.D. wondered how long it would be before she was allowed to take her hands back, but her mother let go first. "There's something I've been wanting to give you," she said, leading J.D. over to the desk. "I know I have it in here, somewhere . . ." As she was rummaging through the desk drawer, J.D.'s gaze wandered around the office. The walls were lined with bookshelves and — at least on the one closest to her — the books were all in alphabetical order. The desk was just as clean as every other surface of the house, the long wooden tabletop holding only a crystal paperweight, a desk calendar, and a computer with an oversized flat monitor.

The screen saver pulsed in a rainbow of colors, exploding out from a point at the center, undulating across the screen, then fading out at the edges, like ripples in a pond. Green fading into blue, which morphed to purple and then green again, the pattern smooth, rhythmic, comforting . . .

J.D. suddenly got the strong urge to look away from the screen — and discovered that she couldn't. It was drawing her in, the swirling colors massaging her mind. Bliss descended from nowhere, suffusing everything with a warm, golden light. *Nothing matters*, the colors said, pulsing, shifting, fading, pulsing, again, again, their rhythm matching the rise and fall of her lungs, the beating of her heart, even the blood coursing through her body. *Calm. Content. Happy.*

J.D. felt a smile spread across her face — but in her mind, a scream echoed, as part of her battled to move, to shut her eyes, to speak, to do *anything* other than stand frozen in place, staring at the colors, letting them take over. A battle waged inside her head, and she was losing, because the flood of contentment drove her back, washed over her, carried her away. And it was so tempting to just let it happen.

"No!" she spit out, wrenching her mouth open with all the will she had left and forcing the sound through her lips. It was supposed to be a scream — it came out a whimper. But still, it was enough, a tiny crack in the wall separating her from herself, and she smashed through it, forcing her gaze away from the screen.

"Honey?" her mother asked, sounding concerned. "Are you okay?"

Knowing it was a bad idea, but knowing she had to try, J.D. stole another look at the monitor, holding her breath. Nothing. It was just a screen saver, colors flashing on and off. Whatever had just happened — it was all in her head.

"Alexa?" her mother asked, hurrying to her side. "What is it? What happened?"

"Nothing," J.D. said quickly.

"You looked a little lost for a moment," her mother prodded. "Like your mind had gone . . . elsewhere?"

J.D. shook her head. "No," she said firmly. "I'm fine. I was just thinking."

It was obvious her mother didn't believe her, but she didn't push it. Instead, she handed J.D. a small black velvet box.

"What's this?" J.D. asked.

"Open it."

J.D. opened the box — and gasped. "It's beautiful." Inside, a delicate silver chain lay on a bed of black velvet. The chain was threaded through a thin silver heart the size of a penny and no thicker than a couple sheets of paper. J.D. touched it hesitantly, then looked back up at her mother. "For me?"

Her mother nodded.

"Why?"

"I was saving this for your birthday, but then you disappeared and I thought . . ." She was silent for a moment. When she continued, her voice was steadier. "I didn't want to wait anymore. Besides, now you have something that reminds you of how much I care about you."

"I know you do," J.D. mumbled.

"Not just in the past, Alexa," her mother insisted. "Not just for all those years you don't remember, but *now*. I care about the person you are right now. And that will be true — whatever happens."

It was as if, somehow, she had known exactly how it felt, worrying that this woman only wanted the daughter that J.D. hadn't figured out how to be. J.D. didn't believe her. Of course she wanted Alexa back. How could she love J.D., who hated her favorite foods and didn't know where the bathroom was in her own house? She didn't even *know* J.D. — any more than J.D. knew her.

But still, there was something comforting in the words. Or at least something comforting about the fact that her mom had known they were needed. As if she understood. Just like a mother.

Her pajamas felt like silk although, according to the tag, they were made out of cotton and polyester. They were pink.

A lot of things in her room were pink: the puffy down comforter, the flowery calendar hanging over the desk, the pillows lining the window seat, six of the shirts hanging in the closet, two of the skirts, and four of the pairs of socks she had found in the top dresser drawer. A fifth pair was a painfully bright orangey-red that almost counted.

At first, J.D. had felt a little strange picking through the drawers, examining the clothes and the jewelry, peeking under the bed and into the back of the closet — she felt like a spy invading someone else's life. But after a while, it got easier. She realized that no one was going to barge through the door and bust her for snooping. This was her room; these were her belongings. Even if they all still felt like they belonged to someone else. Someone kind of . . . well . . . *lame*.

A shelf in the corner was stuffed with books — one was about a clumsy girl who wanted to be a cheerleader, another about a shy girl whose best friend ditched her for the popular crowd. Most were pink; they all looked like they had happy endings. J.D. couldn't remember reading any of them — and couldn't imagine wanting to.

On the bottom shelf, there was a small, lavender book with a heart on the cover and a lock on the side. The spine read "My Diary," and the lock was open. J.D. ran her finger across the bumpy lettering and glanced behind her, making sure she was still alone in the room. Then she reminded herself, this was *her* diary. And she opened it eagerly, hoping that maybe seeing her story unfold in her own voice might bring it all back to her.

March 14
Dear Diary,
Meat loaf for dinner again tonight. Vomit.
But at least Mom only made me eat half of it.
I'm still mad that she won't let me go to the
concert tomorrow. So what if it's a school
night? Everyone else gets to go. Not that

Mom cares. She always says, "Everyone else isn't my daughter. You are." She just doesn't get it.
Love,

Alexa

March 20
I think I failed my English test. Guess that's what happens when you don't study. But is it my fault that Tara was having a crisis? I was up all night IM'ing with her. And then when she came to school the next morning, the zit wasn't even that big! So she was freaking out for nothing, and now we both bombed the test. She's pretty sure her parents will ground her if she brings home another bad grade. At least I don't have to worry about that. Mom's uptight about a lot of stuff, but at least she's not big on the punishment thing. It's kind of cool the way she talks to me like I'm a grown-up, instead of just bossing me around.
Sincerely,

A.C.

March 24,

Sarah invited me to her birthday party! I
thought SHE thought I was a total loser.
I guess not. I hear there's going to be a dj,
and Mom says I can get a new outfit. She's
taking me, Tara, and Amy shopping this weekend, so we can all find the perfect thing to
wear. Just one problem. Karen's not invited. I
didn't tell her that I was, but it's not like I can
keep it a secret. She always says she hates
Sarah, but I know she doesn't mean it. What
if she's mad at me for getting invited? Or what
if she asks me not to go?! Mom says I should
just tell her the truth, and I know she's right.
But when she called tonight, I pretended I was
on the other line. Does that make me a wimp?
Yours till Niagara Falls,

Alexa

There were ten or fifteen more pages like that,
excited descriptions of parties and shopping trips,
complaints about homework, worries about this
friend not speaking to that one, or about whether her
favorite shirt, the one with the flowers on it, was too
lame to wear to school anymore. Each entry was signed

with a different signature — and even the handwriting shifted from page to page — as if the writer had been testing out different identities, trying to find the one that looked best in ink. After May 4, the rest of the book was blank. The diary had been abandoned months ago.

J.D. put down the book. The life that the words — *her* words — described sounded so *normal*, the concerns so simple, she couldn't imagine what it must have been like. And she couldn't imagine what it would be like to be that person again. How had the girl who'd written those entries ended up unconscious on a city street, hours away from her home?

Nor did any of it match up to her nightmares — or her *visions* — the ones that felt so real. There were no explosions, no creepy old man telling her what to destroy. It was all so normal — which should have made her feel better.

"You're home now," her mother had said at dinner. "Whatever happened, it doesn't matter. Just try to forget about it." But that was the whole problem — she already had.

J.D. examined the bulletin board over the desk. It was covered in photos, pictures of girls mugging for the camera. J.D. couldn't find herself in any of them.

In the morning, she decided, she would ask her mother about her friends. Karen, Tara, Amy, Sarah. She rolled the names over in her mind, trying to match them to the faces in the snapshots. Was Karen the short red-headed girl, jumping on a bed in one picture, walking on her hands in another? Was Amy the quiet, dark-haired one who always seemed to be standing at the edge of the photo, as if hoping to disappear beyond the frame? Or was that Tara? But J.D.'s mental dictionary only had one image under the entry for "friend": Daniel. Judging from the photos, she'd known these girls for years, while she'd known Daniel for only a few days, but . . .

The thought slipped away as her gaze fell on the final photo. This one wasn't stuck to the board with a bright pink pushpin. It was propped up in the corner of her desk, in a pale blue frame. The photo showed a man with light brown hair sitting in a chair, cradling a baby in her arms. The man didn't seem aware of the camera; he was focused on the baby, his hand resting atop her thin blond hair. He wasn't smiling, not exactly, but J.D. could somehow tell that he was deeply happy — more than that, content.

My father, she thought, trying to figure out what she was feeling. It wasn't sorrow or grief, but it wasn't quite the same detachment she felt when looking at the pictures of her friends. Had she stared at this picture some nights, wishing he were alive to hold her again? J.D. touched his face lightly, careful not to smudge the glass, and wondered what he would think of a daughter who didn't remember him.

"Alexa?" There was a light knock at the door and then, without waiting for an answer, her mother stepped inside.

Feeling like she'd been caught, J.D. dropped the photo to the desk and whirled around. "I was just, uh, looking around," she said quickly. "Just trying to — you know. Remember."

Her mother nodded. "Of course. That's good. Is there anything . . . anything you want to ask?"

There were a million things. But she still felt weird about opening up in front of this woman she barely knew. J.D. thought of the diary entries, and the way Alexa had so easily asked her mother for advice. She was sure there'd been no awkward silences, no fear of saying the wrong thing or guilt about not saying enough. Her mother had just been "Mom," who cooked meat loaf and rarely yelled.

She picked up the photo again, handing it to her mother. "This is my father, right?"

Her mother's face lit up. "You recognize him?"

J.D. shook her head. "I don't think so. I just . . . you know, figured."

"This is him," her mother said, running her fingers over the photo just like J.D. had done a few minutes before. "I took this a few weeks after bringing you home from the hospital. We were so happy. . . ." She gave herself a little shake, then put the frame back down on the desk. "It's late," she said, "and you must be tired. I just wanted to say good night before you went to sleep."

"Good night," J.D. said softly. "Thank you for . . ." She wanted to say thank you for the large dinner and the soft bed, the roomful of clothes and books and everything else that was so much more than the thin mattress and half-empty locker she'd had at the Center. But she guessed that would be yet another wrong thing to say. "Finding me," she concluded.

Her mother wrapped her in a tight hug. "Thank you for being okay, Alexa. I don't know what I would have done if anything had —" She pressed her head into J.D.'s shoulder and squeezed tight. "I love you, sweetie, just remember that."

J.D. got into bed, and her mother tucked her under the pink covers. "I used to do this when you were little," she said fondly. "But you haven't let me do it in years." She brushed a hand across J.D.'s forehead. "Do you need anything?"

"Well . . ." J.D. wanted to ask, but wasn't sure she should.

"What? Anything."

"It's just . . . do you think you could . . ."

"Honey, what is it?"

"I don't feel like Alexa," she admitted. "I don't remember anything about what it was like to be her. And when you call me that name, it just feels . . ."

"You want me to call you J.D.?" her mother asked, her mouth crumpling.

"Not forever," J.D. said quickly. "Just . . . just until things aren't so weird. Until I —" She wanted to say *until I remember*, but sometimes, most times, she couldn't believe that would ever happen. The blackness of her mind seemed impenetrable. "For now. Is that okay?"

"For now." Her mother nodded, pausing with her head bowed and her hair falling across her face so that J.D. couldn't see her expression. Then she turned away. "Good night . . . J.D." She walked to the door and flicked off the light switch.

As the darkness fell and her mother's footsteps

disappeared down the hall, J.D. made a sudden decision. "Mom?" she called — and in the darkness, the voice sounded like it belonged to someone else. Alexa.

The footsteps returned.

"You called me Mom," the woman said from the doorway. "You don't have to . . . I mean, I'm glad that you feel . . . but I don't want to pressure you."

"It's okay." J.D. could see her silhouetted against the light streaming in from the hallway. She was leaning against the frame, her head tipped to one side, waiting. "About the doctor. That psychiatrist you were talking about? I think I should go. I mean, if you think it's a good idea."

"Are you sure?"

"I'm sure." It wasn't because of the weird visions or hallucinations or flashbacks or whatever they were. It wasn't the terrifying numbness that had come over her earlier that night in her mother's office or the music in her head or the way she'd lost control with Mel, with Daniel. It wasn't even the nightmares that, even here, in this perfect pink room, made her fear falling asleep. It was the knowledge that something — her *life* — had been stolen from her and she was determined to get it back.

sleep

She waits in line. She does not speak to the other girls. Their pale blue jumpsuits match her own, and they all stare straight ahead. The line moves slowly, but eventually she reaches the front. The man with the cruel eyes hands her two pills. They taste bitter, and she wants to spit them out, but he is watching. She swallows. The walls are white and empty. There are no windows. The man hands the pills to the next girl. She shakes her head. "No," the girl says. "Yes," the man says. His voice is familiar; it is a voice to obey. The girl's voice quavers. "No." The man frowns and pulls something from his pocket. He smiles.

And the girl begins to scream.

J.D. woke up with tears running down her cheeks. For a moment, she thought she could still hear the girl's screams. She sat up and drew the blanket around her shoulders, realizing she was shivering. Why did she keep dreaming about that horrible man? And where was that place? It had seemed a little like the hospital and a little like the Center — but not completely like either of them. It was somehow more terrifying, with its windowless walls and its rows of zombie-faced girls. *It was just a dream*, she reminded herself. *Just a dream*. She didn't want that place to be a part of her life, didn't want to imagine that she had ever actually been there, standing in that line, swallowing those pills.

She didn't want to imagine what could have caused those terrifying screams.

The sky was gray with the first light of dawn. It filled her room with shadows. Her heart wouldn't stop racing. J.D. stretched her hand beneath her pillow and pulled out the small silver lock pick and tension wrench Daniel had left for her. She pressed them between her palms, feeling the metal gradually warm beneath her touch. It was the only thing that seemed real.

She lay in bed with her eyes open for a long time, trying to calm her breathing and let herself fall back to sleep. It didn't work. So she got out of bed and walked over to her bureau, where the small velvet box sat on the corner of her dresser. J.D. pulled out the necklace that her mother had given her and slid the heart charm off the thin silver chain. Then she threaded the chain through a small hole at the base of each lock pick and fastened it around her neck. That was a little better.

Then she pulled off the fancy pajamas that smelled like fresh flowers and put on the scratchy green ones she had worn at the Center. That was better, too. As she crawled back under the blanket, J.D. forced herself not to worry about falling asleep and having another nightmare — or about what the morning would bring. The ugly, coarse pajamas reminded her that she could be as strong as she needed to be. And the metal pressing against her chest reminded her that she wasn't alone.

"Are you ready?" her mother asked, pulling the car into a parking space. She shut off the ignition and glanced over at J.D., who nodded.

"Let's do this," she said, surprised to find that she wasn't nervous at all. Maybe it was the setting. She had expected another hospital, but instead, they had driven to a small commercial complex only a few minutes away from the house. It was technically a strip mall, but the builders had obviously done everything in their power to disguise that fact. Ruffled gift stores pressed up against cozy bakeries and cafés; a few children clustered outside the ice-cream shop, their faces smeared with chocolate; low-hanging tree branches kissed the brick facades; and a cobblestone path traveled along the edge of the parking lot. It looked like the kind of place where nothing out of the ordinary would be allowed to happen.

They followed the fake cobblestones to an unmarked door lodged between a pizza place and a yarn store.

"This is a doctor's office?" J.D. asked, pausing in the doorway. "Where's the sign?"

"Many of Dr. Styron's patients prefer to remain discreet," her mother explained. "He finds it's best not to advertise his presence. His patients know where to find him."

J.D. sighed and stepped inside, a patient once again. A long narrow hallway painted in soothing blue led to a small waiting room. The woman behind the receptionist's desk was laying out a game of solitaire across her desk. A man with bushy gray eyebrows, a crooked, bulbous nose, and a cruel smile stood in the middle of the room. The man from her nightmares.

J.D. gasped. Everything in her said *run*, but her mother's grip on her shoulder had tightened. J.D. barely noticed her, or the receptionist — she felt like she was alone in the room with the man. His eyes were black and piercing, flashing in the light. He looked hungry, and she could imagine him rubbing his hands together, licking his lips, eager to consume her. He spoke, and she didn't register the words, only the voice. The low, velvety voice that made her want to claw her ears off to make it stop. It was the voice she'd heard in her mind.

And if it was real — if *he* was real — did that mean the rest of it was, too?

For a moment, she felt like she was back in the nightmare again, unable to move or to scream. But then her mouth opened on command. And as it did, her terror shifted to anger.

No, not anger. Fury. "You," she said, shrugging off her mother's grip and taking a step forward.

He let out a quick gasp and stepped back, surprise and then fear flashing across his face. Their eyes locked, and J.D. felt a surge of power, as if she could destroy him with the force of her hatred, as if she could *think* him into defeat. He stared back, no longer afraid, but defiant, daring her to act. Her hands clenched into fists. Time slowed, and she could feel every second tick past. She watched the rise and fall of his chest, willing it to stop — willing him to disappear.

"Alexa?" A soft hand on her back. "J.D.?"

The connection between them broke; J.D. looked away first.

"J.D., hon, are you okay?" her mother asked anxiously.

"He's . . . he —" She didn't know how to explain.

And when J.D. looked back at the doctor, everything had changed. His face was the same, but the smile seemed gentle now, his eyes soft and inviting. Laugh lines creased his skin, and as he rubbed his bald spot and waggled his eyebrows at her, she realized he looked like someone's grandfather. Just a harmless old man, a family friend.

"Do you recognize me, Alexa?" he asked, and the voice still made her shiver, even though it was nothing but kind.

"My name is J.D.," she said automatically.

He made a small disapproving noise, then nodded. "Do you recognize me?" he repeated.

There was something about him that made her want to tell the truth. "I've seen you in my . . . I think I had a dream where you were . . ."

"What do you remember, J.D.?" her mother pressed.

"I don't remember him, not really," J.D. said. "Just . . . his face. And his voice."

"This could be a good sign," Dr. Styron said. "If you're having dreams about people from your past, it does suggest that your memories are still intact, deep within your mind. Hopefully, once we do a little digging, we'll be able to bring them back to the surface." He frowned. "Of course, dreams are not memories, and the sleeping brain can create all sorts of fanciful scenarios. You probably don't need me to tell you that you can't believe everything you see and hear in your sleep."

J.D. liked the way he spoke to her, rather than to her mother, like she was the one in charge.

"You said this *could* be a good sign," her mother said suddenly. "Does that mean . . . ?"

"The brain is a tricky thing," Dr. Styron admitted. "You have to understand that in cases like this, the brain is fighting a battle against itself, and sometimes that can mean collateral damage."

"What kind of damage?" J.D. asked nervously.

"Oh, in extreme cases, vivid nightmares masquerading as memories, waking delusions, auditory or visual hallucination." Dr. Styron peered down at her intensely. "It's one of the reasons we try not to push too hard. It's imperative not to force the brain to remember before it's ready, or the mind tries to create an alternate reality to supplant the missing past."

J.D.'s mother patted her on the shoulder. "Is there anything you want to tell us?" she asked. "Any . . . symptoms?"

J.D. shook her head.

"Almost certainly none of this applies to J.D.," the doctor said, with forced cheerfulness. "I'm sure we'll have her fixed up in no time."

"But what if . . ." J.D. almost didn't want to know. But she had to. "What if all that stuff you said, what if it starts happening, and I — you know."

"Go crazy?" Dr. Styron asked. He narrowed his eyes for a moment, then frowned. "I'm going to be honest with you, Alexa. When dealing with this kind of situation, severe mental deterioration is always a concern. It's one of the reasons I suggested your mother bring you in, so we could work through this together. But I don't want you to worry. If something goes wrong — it's a very small chance, but if — that's not the end of the story. I know of an excellent rehabilitation center where they specialize in this kind of thing, where patients receive top-notch, round-the-clock care and supervision."

"You would send me away?" J.D. asked in a small voice. She didn't realize how much she'd gotten used to the idea of being *home* — not until they threatened to take it away from her. She glanced over at her mother, who gave her a sad smile. *I don't want to leave her,* J.D. realized in surprise. *Not now — not when I'm just starting to know her.*

"You really don't need to worry about that right now," Dr. Styron assured her. "There's every indication that you'll be able to recover at home, with your mother. We'll do whatever we can to get you well again. That's what you want, isn't it?"

J.D. nodded, wondering what would happen if she confessed right then about her visions, her hallucinations, her . . . episodes. It sounded like he would haul out the straitjacket and stick her on the next bus to the mental institution, some dingy prison with bars on the windows and padded walls. Once they locked you up in a place like that, did they ever let you out?

Maybe she belonged in a place like that. But J.D. refused to believe it. She had only just found her mother, her home — and she wanted a chance to find *herself.* So she couldn't tell them the truth about what was going on inside her head. She just had to get a grip.

Her mother didn't want to stay out in the waiting room but, in the end, Dr. Styron insisted. His office had a couch and a chair, and he told J.D. she was free to choose between them. She picked the chair.

Dr. Styron pulled his own chair out from behind his desk and planted it across from hers. He sat down and opened his notebook to a fresh page.

J.D. hunched forward in the chair, waiting for him to speak.

There was an awkward pause.

"Do I make you nervous?" Dr. Styron asked.

"What? No. Why?"

"You seem a little tense."

"You'd be tense, too, if you got dumped in the middle of someone else's life," J.D. shot back. "I'm sorry. I just meant, this is all kind of weird for me. It's not you." Although it still was, a little. "Things are just pretty weird right now." She slumped down in the chair, feeling a sudden hopelessness wash over her. What if Dr. Styron couldn't help her and things were like this forever?

"Perhaps hearing some music would help you relax a bit," Dr. Styron suggested. "Would you like that?"

J.D. shrugged. "I guess."

He flipped through a CD case and stuck a disc into the stereo, pressing play. J.D.'s eyes widened as the familiar melody trickled over her, this time outside her head. It started happening again, the disturbing out-of-body sensation that carried her mind up and away, as if she were watching the scene happen to someone else, as if someone else were in control. The music's hold over her was weaker than before, and she knew that if she struggled against it, pushed back against the flow, she could regain control. Or she could let it sweep her away. It would be so easy. . . .

"No!" J.D. wrenched herself out of the trance and snapped back into the moment. Dr. Styron turned off the music and looked at her with naked curiosity. Not worry or alarm, just a questioning stare.

"What is it?"

"Nothing," she said quickly.

"That's not true," he told her. "Something happened

when I turned on the music. You went somewhere else for a moment. And then you shouted."

"It was *nothing*," she insisted.

His hand hovered over the stereo. "I could turn on the music again."

"I just got distracted," she said quickly, desperate to keep him from pressing play. "Something about the song — it's just something I've heard before, and I was trying to figure out where."

Dr. Styron sat down again. "I don't think that's it," he said sternly. "I think that music made you feel like you weren't in control of yourself anymore — that you were watching yourself from very far away. Almost like you were two different people. Am I in the ballpark?"

She couldn't believe it. "How did you know?"

He sighed. "I was afraid of this. Sometimes, when the brain is under great stress, it can compensate by isolating the problem. Essentially creating a new personality with none of the stresses and strains of the old. Do you understand what I'm trying to say?"

"Sort of." She hesitated. "But I don't feel like two personalities. I just feel like me."

"Like J.D., right?"

"Yes."

"But you're *not* J.D.," he pointed out. "You're Alexa Collins. And yet you insist on calling yourself by this other name, pretending that you have no connection to the person that you used to be. I would guess that in your mind, you think of that self as if she's another person."

J.D. tried not to react, but she knew Dr. Styron was right — Alexa didn't feel like a part of her.

"Don't be alarmed," Dr. Styron said, but his tone wasn't very convincing. "Obviously you've still got a firm grip on reality. You *know* that you are Alexa Collins, you just don't *feel* it, right?"

"I'm trying," J.D. protested. "I really am."

"But are you?" Dr. Styron pressed. "You still call yourself J.D."

J.D. didn't know what to say.

"I know that you *think* you want to get your memory back," Dr. Styron said. "And I'm sure that a part of you does. But there's another part of you that's fighting against remembering. Something in your mind is suppressing those memories, and we don't know why yet. So as we struggle to heal you, a part of you is battling against us. The longer this goes on, the stronger that part gets. The tighter you hold on to this J.D. persona you've created, the harder it will be to rescue Alexa, wherever she's gone."

"It's not a persona," J.D. protested. "It's me."

"I know it seems that way. But what does it mean to say, 'That's me'? After all, what is the self, other than an accumulation of memories? We are who we are because of what has happened to us, wouldn't you say?"

J.D. made a weak noise of agreement.

"And you don't remember anything that's happened to you before you were 'J.D.' So in a very real, very dangerous way, J.D. and Alexa *are* two different people. It's our job to make them one again. But if that's going to happen, you're going to have to commit yourself to getting better. You *do* want to get better, don't you?"

J.D. thought about everything that had happened to her in the last few days — the explosion, the hospital, the Center, the fight, the visions. Why was she clinging to that life? *Alexa* didn't have those problems. *Alexa* had a mother sitting out in the waiting room who would do anything for her. She had her own room, warm bed, clothes to wear, people who cared about her. Everything the kids in the Center didn't have.

Everything Daniel didn't have.

Her fingers skimmed across the thin silver bars hanging from her neck. Then she nodded firmly. "Yes," she said, sitting up straight in the chair. "I want to get better. What do I have to do?"

J.D. lay on the couch, her head resting on a stiff, flat pillow. Dr. Styron's face loomed over her.

"Relax," he instructed. "I'll guide your unconscious mind into the past, and this will help us figure out what's going on in there." He leaned over and tapped her forehead lightly. "Then gradually we should be able to reintegrate your subconscious memories with your conscious ones. It's as simple as that."

"Will it . . . hurt?"

He laughed. "Of course not. It will just feel like you're going to sleep. I'll ask you some questions, and you'll be able to answer me from a place beneath your conscious mind. We'll only do a little today, then I'll bring you out of it. You won't remember a thing."

It was the worst thing he could have said.

"Are you ready?"

"Not really," she admitted. "But okay."

"Close your eyes and try to relax."

She was sure it wasn't going to work. She felt like she did at night, her muscles clenched and her mind racing, waiting for something terrible to strike. But as she listened to Dr. Styron's voice rising and falling, the soothing rhythm ebbing and flowing in time with her breathing, urging her to relax her neck, relax her shoulders, relax her legs, relax her mind, she felt a deep contentment settle over her, an almost physical weight that blanketed the fear and worry with a warm, fuzzy layer of calm and peace.

"Deeper and deeper," he murmured. "Hear the sound of my voice, guiding you down, into the darkness . . ."

In her mind, she took a step down, then another, and then the darkness swallowed her up.

"Okay, Alexa, you may wake up now."

"What?" J.D. opened her eyes and sat up. "It didn't work?"

"It worked perfectly," Dr. Styron said. "We made some good progress. This was a very promising start."

"But I didn't . . . I just closed my eyes," J.D. protested.

Dr. Styron tapped his watch. "That was an hour ago."

A familiar emptiness opened inside of her — more time lost, more moments forgotten.

"So what did I say?" she asked.

"It would be very counterproductive for us to discuss that," he said. "You're not ready to absorb these memories into your conscious mind."

She hated the not knowing but even more, she hated the fact that he knew more about her than she knew about herself. And suddenly, too late, it occurred to her to wonder, what if she had said something about all the strange things that had been happening? What if Dr. Styron now realized how much worse things were than he had thought?

"I didn't say anything that, um, made you think I was, you know, damaged? Like you said before?" she asked nervously.

He gave her a reassuring smile. "Nothing of the sort," he said. "In fact, after today's session, I feel more strongly than ever that things are going to proceed exactly as planned."

trust

She couldn't start calling herself Alexa. Not out loud, not inside her head. And she couldn't let anyone else do it, either. But she did her best to follow the rest of Dr. Styron's instructions. She spent hours on the couch next to her mother, poring through old photo albums and learning about herself.

"This was your first trip to the zoo, and all you wanted to see were the penguins. Every time we tried to take you out of the penguin house to see something else, you started screaming."

The page turned.

"This was your first birthday party after your father . . . after he was gone, and I wanted to make it special for you. That's why there are so many presents. You looked so happy that day, but later, I found you up in your bedroom, crying — and you said you were only pretending to be happy to make Mommy feel better. You were always so sweet and thoughtful like that."

"This was the summer you learned how to swim. I couldn't get you to come out of the water."

"This is you accepting a sportsmanship award at your first summer camp."

"This is you . . ."

"This is you . . ."

"This is you."

Each time her mother turned the page, J.D. thought, maybe the next photo, maybe the next image would match one in her head. It never happened. But she did like cuddling up against her mother on the couch, her mother's arm around her shoulders, their heads pressed together over the album. That felt right, even if nothing else did.

She sat in Alexa's room that night, trying to persuade herself that it belonged to her. She listened to Alexa's favorite songs, ate Alexa's favorite foods, wore Alexa's favorite clothes, and waited to turn back into Alexa. She lay in bed at night, telling herself stories from the past, anecdotes about arguments and parties and sleepovers that she had picked up from her journal. "Remember the time Tara and I were roasting marshmallows and almost lit our hair on fire?" she silently asked herself. But the answer was no.

Twice the next day, she returned to Dr. Styron's office, lay down on his couch, and let him lull her to sleep. He said she was making excellent progress, no matter how she felt.

At least the dreams stopped.

Once the hypnotherapy sessions had begun, the nightmares ended. And as far as J.D. was concerned, that was reason enough to keep them up. But if the nights were shorter, the days were endless. Other than her sessions with Dr. Styron, J.D. wasn't allowed to leave the house — for her own good. That meant no trips . . . and no visitors.

After two days, she couldn't stand it anymore. "Wouldn't it be good for me to meet some of Alexa's — I mean, my friends?" J.D. asked her mother. "If I'm supposed to surround myself with familiar things, wouldn't that help?"

"I don't think so, honey," her mother replied. "We don't want to overstimulate you right now, and . . ."

"And what?"

"Your condition might be a little unsettling for

your friends," her mother said, a note of apology in her voice.

It didn't matter. J.D. didn't have much interest in meeting those girls. From what she'd picked up from the pictures, the notes, and the journal entries, they were giggly and shallow. And while Alexa may have had plenty in common with them, J.D. was sure that *she* didn't. What would they talk about? The sound Mel's head had made slamming against the pavement, or the way the girls at the Center cried themselves to sleep at night? The way it felt to lie chained to a hospital bed, not knowing who you were or how you got there? Would she confide in them about her waking nightmares, the dark visions that haunted her brain and felt like the only true memories she had?

J.D. guessed not. If anything, they would probably pester her for gossipy details, just like the reporters who occasionally lurked outside the house. And she could do without that.

"What about Daniel?" J.D. asked.

Her mother heaved a sigh. "I've already told you, Dr. Styron thinks it's best for you to make a fresh start, and I agree with him."

"I just want to email him," J.D. argued. "What's wrong with that?"

"Maybe in a few days, hon. Try to be patient."

J.D. balled up her fists. Her mother just didn't get it. J.D. was trying so hard to be the perfect daughter, the perfect patient. She didn't complain. She did everything she was told. All she wanted was to talk to Daniel — and suddenly, she realized she wanted it desperately. "But he's going to think I forgot about him!" she shouted, flinging her arms out in frustration.

Her mother jerked backward, almost as if . . . almost as if she was afraid, J.D. thought.

"Calm down." Her mother's voice lacked its usual smooth certainty.

She's scared of me, J.D. realized. *But why?*

"I am calm," she said, extremely un-calmly. "I just need you to understand —"

"I get it," her mother said. "I do." And now she'd backed up so far she was pressed against the wall. J.D. had seen that look before — at the Center, after the fight with Mel. After Mel's head had smacked into the pavement, the kids had all looked at her that way: wary. Afraid. She hadn't liked it then, but it had worked to her advantage. Now?

J.D. wondered if she could use it again and *make* her mother give in.

She hated herself for even having the thought. She wasn't that person. J.D. had never meant to hurt Mel; she didn't want to hurt anyone. And her mother, of all people, was supposed to know that. Her mother was supposed to look at her with love and understanding . . . not fear.

"It's okay," J.D. said quietly. "I understand."

"I just want what's best for you," her mother said.

J.D. nodded and kept her eyes on the floor. "I know." She didn't want to see her mother's face again, not until she was sure that look was gone.

"He won't think you've forgotten him," her mother assured her. "He can wait a few more days." J.D. felt a hand on her shoulder. She took a deep breath and looked up. Her mother was smiling, her eyes warm.

J.D. didn't ask about Daniel again.

But she couldn't forget him, or her need to talk to him. Daniel was her lifeline. He was the only one who knew everything about her, the *real* her, not the one who was putting on a performance, pretending to be Alexa. Pretending to be normal. Daniel knew what was really going on — and even though he knew, he didn't think she was crazy. J.D. needed that reassurance. She needed someone she could be honest with.

And she needed to get back in touch with him *before* her memories returned, if they ever did. Because Daniel was J.D.'s best friend — her only friend. But to Alexa, he might just be some boy she'd met in another life. J.D. worried about losing him almost as much as she worried about losing herself. And she was afraid that if she didn't make contact soon, it would be that much easier for him to disappear. So that night, when the house was silent and her mother was sound asleep, J.D. snuck out of her bedroom and down the hall. Telling herself this was better than risking another argument, she opened the door to her mother's study and stepped inside.

It was easy enough to find the web browser on her mother's computer, and she quickly logged into her account.

There was one message waiting for her. It was from dannyboy16.

Just wanted to say hi. Hope you like it at home. Remember anything yet? Kendall got locked in the bathroom last night. He was banging on the door for an hour before someone heard and let him out. Very embarrassing. Wonder how that happened?

:)

D

The hallway creaked.

J.D. froze, holding her breath. She stared at the heavy wooden door, waiting for it to swing open. What would her punishment be?

She told herself she didn't care. This had been worth it. But she still held as still and silent as possible, terrified of getting caught. Minutes passed. Nothing happened. She waited. Still nothing.

Eventually, gathering her courage, J.D. crept slowly toward the door and, taking a deep breath, poked her head into the hall. It was empty. Her head tipped back as she sighed with relief.

She considered going back to bed — next time, it might not be a phantom creak. Next time, it might be her mother.

But she couldn't leave without emailing Daniel back. She couldn't let him think that she had forgotten him.

Home is weird, she typed, pressing gently on each key so it would make the softest possible click. But good, I guess. My mother is nice. And there's this doctor — he's helping me. No more nightmares!

J.D.

PS Better keep out of Kendall's way now that you don't have a girl to protect you. :)

She went to hit SEND, then paused, and added another line.

PPS Miss you.

The sessions with Dr. Styron always began the same way. They would sit down across from each other as they had that first time, and Dr. Styron would ask the same series of questions. Had she experienced any strange or disturbing symptoms? Had there been any odd events, moments she couldn't explain? Had she experienced visual or auditory hallucinations? Delusions of grandeur or the irrational belief that she had caused things beyond her control? Had she felt she was growing distant from herself, or splitting into two people again? Had she lost control of her body or blacked out? Had she suffered sensations or emotions that seemed imposed on her mind from somewhere else?

And because the nightmares had stopped, along with the hallucinations and the blackouts and all the other terrifying episodes, she was always able to say, truthfully, "No." She was getting better.

He never asked whether she remembered anything.

She would lie down on the couch, close her eyes, listen to his voice — and then wake up what seemed like a moment later, remembering nothing.

"Excellent progress today," he said at the end of the session, the final element of the ritual.

J.D. stood up and pulled on her sweatshirt. "Guess I'll see you tomorrow," she said. "Eleven thirty again?"

"Actually, I think it would be best for you to come in earlier, around nine," he told her. "I've already spoken to your mother."

"A longer session?" she asked. "Are you sure —" She broke off, her eyes fixed on his shoes. Black, shiny, patent leather loafers with a gold bar running across the top of each one. She didn't know why the sight of them made her chest tighten or why she suddenly felt the need to flee. But she couldn't stop staring at them.

The room is pure white, empty. But the flashing lights give everything a glow. Green fades to blue, then purple, then green. She sits perfectly still. The straps bind her wrists to the chair, but she does not struggle. She does not care. She is at peace. Dr. Styron stands beside her. The needle slides into her skin. The pain seems very far away. She smiles as the pale green liquid seeps into her arm. "Do you understand the instructions?" Dr. Styron asks. She nods. "And you know what to do?" She nods again. The liquid burns as it spreads through her body. The pain sears her from the inside. She smiles. The lights dance. Dr. Styron nods. "You're ready."

"Ready for what!?" she shrieked, then realized that she was back in Dr. Styron's familiar, cozy office, standing up, free. She blinked hard once, then again, making sure that what she was seeing was real and that the vision wasn't going to come back.

Vision?

Hallucination?

Or memory?

"Calm down, Alexa," Dr. Styron said, crossing

the room toward her. She stepped back quickly, pressing herself against the wall.

"Don't touch me," she hissed, as he reached out a hand.

"What did you see, Alexa?" He spread his hands wide as if to demonstrate there were no concealed weapons. "Take a few deep breaths and tell me about it. What just happened?"

"I saw *you*," she spit out, "and you were —" She didn't know how to finish the thought. None of it made any sense. They were just a jumble of terrifying images that were already fading from her mind. "You were hurting me," she told the doctor, peering into his eyes to find some glimpse of calculating cruelty, some indication that the sweet, comforting expression was just a disguise. But there was nothing. "I was trapped, and I couldn't move, and you were — you were doing *something*."

Dr. Styron smiled and leaned back against his desk. "Is that all? That's quite a good sign, Alexa. We're making more progress than I'd thought."

"What?" Her surprise knocked her anger and fear right out of her head. She had expected him to defend himself or act suspiciously — or declare that she'd totally lost it. Either he was evil or she was crazy, and neither of those two scenarios was a good sign.

"You're getting nervous," he explained. "Or at least, your mind is. This is proof we're on the right track. We're getting closer to whatever it is you're trying so hard not to remember. Your mind has erected a barrier between you and your past, and we're trying to break it down bit by bit. It's only natural for your mind to fight us every step of the way — and now that we're getting close, it's fighting harder. Whatever it is you imagined, it's just a metaphor for that struggle."

"Maybe," she said defiantly. The images had been too vivid, felt too real. "Or *maybe* you've been lying to me this whole time. *What are you doing to me?*"

He sighed. "I had really hoped that by this point, you would have a little more faith in me," he said. "But I suppose trust isn't very fashionable these days. That's why I tape every session."

"What? You do? Why?"

"For legal reasons, of course. And for situations such as this. So if you'd like, I can show you exactly what happens after I put you to sleep and that I am not, in fact, the monster you imagine me to be. If you feel you need that kind of reassurance."

He looked hurt and disappointed. But she couldn't worry about hurting his feelings; she had to worry about herself. "Yes," she said firmly. "I need it."

He ushered her into the hallway. "Wait here." She watched him walk down to the end of the hallway and, pulling a key from his breast pocket, let himself into the door at the end of the hall. She hadn't even noticed it before and wondered what it led to. He was back a moment later, carrying a black laptop. "There's a wireless feed from the camera into my office. I find it's best to keep the computer in a separate room, for security reasons. You never know when a patient's going to want to go nosing around in his file." He laughed to show he was joking, but she didn't join him.

"Okay, then." He carried the computer over to the desk, flipped it open, and double clicked on an icon shaped like an old-time movie camera. Soon, a window popped up on the screen and J.D. saw a frozen image of herself, stretched out on the couch. Dr. Styron hit play.

"Tell me what happened the day of the explosion," the tiny screen version of Dr. Styron asked.

"I don't remember."

J.D. shivered. There was something very creepy

135

about watching herself lie there with her eyes closed, speaking in that slow, steady, emotionless voice — especially since she couldn't remember any of it.

"What's the first thing you do remember?" Dr. Styron asked.

"Waking up on the street," she told him.

"I want you to try something for me. Let's turn back the clock. I want you to go backward in time. Pretend you're watching a movie on rewind. Can you do that for me?"

J.D. said yes in the same emotionless zombie tone.

"So rewind the movie backward in your head. The ambulance is zooming away from you. You're lying on the street alone. You open your eyes. But what happens *before* that?"

His voice was so soothing and rhythmic that, even now, J.D. was mesmerized. On the screen, she spoke.

"I see something," she said.

"Tell me about it."

Dr. Styron clicked the mouse, and the window disappeared. He shut the lid of the laptop.

"Why'd you do that?" J.D. yelped. She had

remembered something! The memories were in her *somewhere* — she needed to see more.

"Watching this any further could be detrimental to your recovery," Dr. Styron said. "We've discussed this before. Frustrating as it may be for you, the things you remember in your unconscious state are things that your conscious mind is not ready to absorb."

"But —"

"Alexa, be reasonable — I can see that watching yourself in the hypnotic state is disturbing you. And that's only natural. But it would be irresponsible for me to subject you to any more of this."

"But those are *my* memories," J.D. protested. "I should get to hear them if I want to. This isn't fair."

"It's not about what's fair," he lectured her. "You have to trust me on this. If we try to push it, well . . . you've already seen how hard your brain is willing to push back. I assume you don't want to have another episode like that — unless, that is, you still believe it was some kind of memory?"

J.D. had gotten so absorbed in the video that she'd almost forgotten why they were watching it. She was still upset that he wouldn't show her more. But at least now she knew what happened after he put her under — and there was a deep relief in that. "No, I believe you." She blushed, feeling kind of stupid for suspecting him of . . . she didn't even know what. Some kind of bizarre evil plan. "Sorry I freaked out. It just seemed so . . . *real*. You know?"

"No offense taken," he assured her. "Just make sure you let me know if it happens again."

"You think it's going to happen again?" she asked in alarm.

There was a long pause.

"It's possible," Dr. Styron admitted. "And frequent episodes of this type would, of course, be troubling. But don't worry." He clapped her heartily on the back and guided her toward the door. "We're keeping a close eye on things. And I'm sure you have nothing to worry about." He said it in a tone she had heard before.

While she was in the hospital, J.D. had overheard Dr. Fisher telling a woman about her husband's injuries. The patient had taken a turn for the worse, the doctor had said, and there were some troubling indications. The woman had started to cry, and the doctor assured her that her husband was being monitored closely, and they had every reason to believe that things would turn around. He assured the woman she probably had nothing to worry about.

The next day, J.D. asked her doctor about the man. He had died just after breakfast.

secrets

She wasn't supposed to leave the house.

But she had to.

After the session, J.D. felt like something was crawling through her brain, jumbling her thoughts and mashing them together until nothing made sense. Only one thought cut through the chaos: She was getting worse.

From what she'd seen on the video, J.D. at least knew that the memories were there, buried somewhere deep inside. It should have been good news. But what if she lost her mind before Dr. Styron was able to fix it?

I'm stronger than that, she told herself. She wouldn't let madness overtake her — she would fight. But how was she supposed to fight her own mind? J.D. squeezed her eyes shut and pressed her lips together. She was determined not to cry. She couldn't afford to lose it, not now. Not when she had to be strong. She would figure this out.

But she couldn't do it shut up in the house — and she couldn't do it alone. She needed Daniel. She needed to see him.

This was more important than following the rules. So that afternoon, while her mother was upstairs working, J.D. opened the door and stepped outside.

There was a train station about a mile from the house — they passed it on the way to Dr. Styron's office. And J.D. knew that, once there, she could catch a train back into the city. She could find the Center. She could find Daniel.

And she could do it all on her own.

There was something exhilarating about being outside alone, and J.D. felt the sudden urge to run. She sprinted down the sidewalk, laughing into the wind. She was running so fast that she didn't even notice the little boy on the tricycle, until he called out to her.

"Hey, you!" he shouted.

J.D. stopped and bent over, lungs heaving. Once she'd caught her breath, she glanced over at the boy. He was five or six, with curly red hair and orange freckles spattered across his face.

"Who are you?" he asked, sounding tough, like he was trying to protect his turf. He pedaled toward her and stopped with the plastic front wheel a few inches from her feet.

"Where are your parents?" she asked, wondering which house he belonged to.

"Inside." He pointed to a house with blue shutters a few yards away. "Where's *your* parents?"

"My mom's in our house, too," she said, hoping he wouldn't ask about her father. His tricycle was red, just like hers had been — at least, according to the pictures. "We live right over there." She pointed down the block.

"Nuh-uh," he argued. "You don't live here."

"Do too." Why she was arguing with a kinder-gartner?

"No one lives there," he said. "My friend Kyle used to live there, but he had to move away some-where stupid."

"Are you sure it was that house?" J.D. asked. "The one with the green mailbox?"

The kid nodded so hard his teeth clattered together. "Kyle still owes me a candy bar from when he bet me that I couldn't stick a bug up my nose. But I could. Wanna see?"

"*No*," J.D. said quickly. "Definitely not." She looked back over her shoulder at her house. The kid must be wrong, she thought. No matter how sure he seemed, he was a six-year-old. What did he know? "I've lived here my whole life."

"I know everyone on this street," he said proudly. Then he scowled at her. "And I don't know you."

"You can't know *everyone* on the street," she pointed out. "That's a lot of people. Some of them must be strangers."

"*You're* a stranger," he said triumphantly. "I'm not supposed to talk to strangers. Are you a bad person?"

J.D. shook her head. "I don't think so."

The kid stared at her for a moment, then he started pedaling his tricycle again, riding around her in narrowing circles. "I think you are," he said. "I think you're a big liar." He looked back toward his house. "Mom!" he shouted suddenly. "A bad stranger is trying to talk to me! Mom! *Mom! Stranger danger!*"

Part of J.D. wanted to stay and talk to his mother, who was sure to come flying out of the house as soon as she heard her child's screams. But before she could get answers, J.D. would have to convince the woman that she wasn't trying to hurt her bratty kid.

There'd probably be a lot of yelling and then a call to J.D.'s mom. And J.D. just wasn't in the mood to deal.

So she ran.

She could have run to the train station but, instead, without thinking, she ran home — home to the house that maybe used to be Kyle's. But probably not, because the kid was just a kid. Sometimes they misunderstood. Sometimes they lied. Sometimes kids were just plain wrong. Just like this one was.

That was the only possible explanation.

Her mother would have the answer, she decided, stepping back into the house. Her mother would know that this Kyle person had lived next door or down the street. She would explain that someone else's house was for sale and had been empty for months, not theirs. She would think J.D. was silly for believing a loudmouthed six-year-old over everything she'd seen and heard. But J.D. was going to ask anyway.

She crossed through the living room and headed for the stairs, then paused, taking a deep breath. There was a wonderful scent in the air, a little sweet, a little spicy, something like . . . gingerbread.

"Swing me again, Mommy!" Her mother picks her up and whirls her through the air as Alexa shrieks with joy. "Again! Again!" she cries, but eventually the ride ends, and her feet land back on the floor. "Is it cookie time yet?"

"Not yet," her mother says. "They need time to cool."

"Okay." Alexa waits a moment. "How about now?"

Her mother laughs. Alexa loves the sound of her mother's laugh, almost as much as she loves gingerbread cookies. She presses against her mother's side, where it is soft and warm. There is a mound of presents under the tree, all for her. But she is not allowed to open them yet. First they will eat gingerbread cookies and watch the sparkling lights on the tree. Then they will sing songs in front of the fire. And then, just before bedtime, Alexa will get to open one present. She already knows which one she will pick. The big one with the gold wrapping paper and the green bow. She can't wait.

Alexa holds her arms out to her mother. "One more time?" she asks.

Her mother giggles. "One more time," she agrees. And she lifts Alexa off the ground and swings her through the air, round and round. It feels like flying.

J.D. realized she was holding her breath. She let it out in a loud whoosh. It had come flooding back to her, just as Dr. Styron had predicted. Not everything — not even most things. But a single memory of her life *before*. She remembered how it felt to be Alexa, to long for her mother to hold her, to be happy.

She *remembered*.

"Mom!" she cried, storming up the stairs. She hurried down the hall. The door to her mother's office was closed, which only happened when she was on the phone or trying to finish an important project. J.D. wasn't supposed to interrupt either one unless it was an emergency. But this definitely qualified as an emergency.

The nightmare was over — or at least ending. It was only a matter of time before everything else came back. She knew it. She paused outside the door, her eyes closed, savoring the sensation of *remembering* something. It was all so clear — the rough texture of her mother's corduroy pants, the way the lights danced on the tree, the Christmas carols wafting through the air — it was as if it had always been a part of her. She couldn't remember *not* remembering it. She had to tell her mother.

She swung the door open quietly, not wanting to disturb a phone call. Her mother was standing in the middle of the room, her back to the door, a cell phone pressed to her ear.

"I agree," her mother said in an unusually tight, businesslike voice. "We can't afford that risk. And the more time that passes . . ." She paused. "You're right. We need to get her to the Institute, and soon."

J.D. gasped. "You're sending me away?"

serenity

Her mother flipped the phone shut and whirled around. "What are you doing in here?" she snapped.

J.D. fought back tears. Now that she was *finally* making some progress, her own mother was giving up? "You were talking about me, weren't you?" she said accusingly. "You want to send me away to some horrible place where I won't bother you anymore? *Sorry*, I didn't know I was so much trouble!" She fled down the hall, refusing to let her mother see the tears.

But her mother followed her and grabbed her from behind, folding her into a tight embrace. "I'm so sorry, honey, you weren't supposed to hear that."

"Obviously," J.D. spat out.

"No. I mean, I didn't want you to find out like that. I wanted to talk to you, to explain what's going on. . . ." She released J.D. from the hug but held her lightly by the shoulders. "That was Dr. Styron on the phone, honey. He told me about what happened at your session today, and he's concerned —"

"But he doesn't have to be!" J.D. exclaimed. "Not anymore. That's what I was coming up here to tell you. I remembered!"

"You did?"

"Well . . . not everything. But I remembered Christmas," J.D. said. "You and me, and a tree."

Her mother sighed. "Oh, J.D., you don't have to start making things up just to make us think you're getting better," she said sadly. "I know you feel like there's a lot of pressure on you, but —"

"I'm *not* making it up," she protested. "When I came inside —"

"You went outside?" Her mother's head jerked back in surprise. "You know you're not supposed to do that. *Ever.*"

"I know. I know. But that's not important — I came inside and I smelled something sweet, like cookies."

"I'm baking gingerbread cookies," her mother said, with a faint smile on her face. "You used to love them."

J.D. nodded eagerly. "Yes, gingerbread cookies, and I remembered. It was Christmas, and there was this big gold present under the tree and you were swinging me around —"

"You *do* remember!" Her mother swept her into another hug, and together they spun in circles, just like they'd done all those years ago. "That was one of our happiest Christmases, sweetie, and I can't believe you —" Her voice broke off, and she lifted an arm to wipe at her eyes. "I was starting to worry that you would never . . . I'm just so happy for you. For us."

"So don't you see?" J.D. said. "I'm getting better. Now I don't have to go anywhere. I can stay here with you."

Her mother's arms fell to her sides and she stepped back. The joyful expression was gone.

"I wish you were right," she said sadly, shaking her head. "But it doesn't change anything. In fact, it makes it all the more important for you to be in a place where they specialize in working with . . ."

"Freaks like me?" J.D. asked bitterly.

"With *memory disorders*. Dr. Styron says —"

"Dr. Styron is a liar!" J.D. cried. She realized she

had nothing left to lose, so she might as well spill everything. "And I had these memories of him — of him telling me to destroy things and explosions and sticking me with some kind of needle, and he told me I was just imagining things — but maybe I wasn't and he just wants to get me out of the way!"

Her mother's eyes had widened in shock. "Oh my god," she said, in a voice only a little louder than a whisper.

J.D. felt the tension leeching out of her body. It felt good to admit her fears out loud — and it felt even better to know that her mother believed her.

"It's worse than I'd thought." Her mother pressed a hand to her lips. "Dr. Styron said severe paranoia, but I never realized it was . . ."

"You don't believe me?" J.D. asked incredulously.

"Believe what? That Dr. Styron is *evil*? Honey, I know it feels real, but these are just symptoms —"

"No!"

"Alexa —"

"*Don't call me that!*" she screamed. "I'm not crazy, I'm not, I'm not, I'm *not*!" She burst into tears and backed away from her mother's arms, pressing herself against the wall, her shoulders shaking and her fore-head resting against the cool paint.

Her mother's fingers skimmed over the back of her neck, then fell away.

"Please. Please don't make me go away. Let me stay here. With you. I'm starting to get better, really I am. I just need more time."

Her mother sighed. "If you really are starting to remember, maybe . . ." she murmured, almost to herself.

"I am," J.D. said eagerly. "I really am."

"And these delusions you're having?"

"Maybe it was a one-time thing," J.D. said. "Dr. Styron himself said he didn't know if it would ever happen again."

"If we gave it a little more time . . ."

J.D. held her breath.

"You would still have to go to your sessions every day. And you have to agree to tell me if you have *any* more symptoms."

"Yes. Yes, of course."

Her mother nodded. "Okay. Dr. Styron won't like it, but . . . we'll give it a few more days. But if . . . if things don't go the way we hope, then you'll agree to go to the Institute? You'll let us help you?"

J.D. was sure that it wouldn't come to that. She *was* getting better. She could feel it. The memories were coming back. So it didn't matter how she answered. "Yes," she said finally. "I'll let you help me. I promise."

"Who wants corn on the cob?" her mother asks. Alexa shoots her hand into the air. Her friends jump up and down. "Me! Me!" they cry.

Dr. Styron mans the grill. "Burgers are almost done," he says, wearing an apron with a giant fish on the front. "First one's for the birthday girl."

"That's me!" Alexa cries. She grabs a plate and holds it out to Dr. Styron. He plops the burger on it, then draws a smiley face with the ketchup. She giggles and takes a big bite. The burger is juicy and sweet, and ketchup runs down her face.

Her mother smears it off with a paper napkin, then gives her a kiss on the forehead.

"I love you, birthday girl."

"I love you, too."

J.D. opened her eyes and wished she could fall back asleep. The dream was already slipping away, along with the deep contentment she'd felt standing in the backyard with everyone in the world she knew and loved. Reality was back — but at least she still had the memory.

Lying there alone in the dark, uncertainty creeped into her. How could she be so sure of herself, when her self was exactly the thing she'd lost?

She felt a burning need to see Daniel. He was the one person who really *knew* her. He couldn't answer her questions, but at least he could stand by her while she searched for herself.

It was three-thirty in the morning. Too late to sneak out of the house. And she was sure that tomorrow, her mother would be watching her constantly. But tomorrow night, after her mother went to bed, J.D. would be free. And Daniel would find a way to sneak out of the Center and meet her, she knew it. All she had to do was ask.

She crept out of bed and down the hallway to her mother's office. But when she sat down at the computer, she stopped cold.

There was a brochure sitting next to the keyboard.

RECOVER YOUR SERENITY AT
THE GREENBOROUGH INSTITUTE

The cover featured a beautiful white mansion sur-rounded by a sprawling green meadow. Tiny figures lounged on the expansive porch, leaning against thick white pillars or lying in hammocks. In the foreground, a group played soccer on the lawn.

It didn't *look* like such a scary place. Maybe Dr. Styron really did want to help her, and maybe he was right that this was the way to do it.

She shook her head, trying to toss out the thought. No. *No.* She wasn't going to be a prisoner some-where, even somewhere as pretty as the Institute. They were plotting against her, trying to make her *think* it was okay, when they really just wanted to —

Wait. Was that paranoia? Or just fear? How was she supposed to know the difference?

She didn't feel crazy. She felt reasonable — if she was afraid, she had a right to be. But . . . wasn't that exactly what a paranoid mental patient would say?

J.D. put the brochure down, careful to place it in exactly the same position. *You are not alone*, it said. That was probably supposed to sound comforting. But it just made her feel like someone was watch-ing her.

And *that* had to be paranoia.

Which meant she was getting worse.

The email was brief:

Daniel — can you get out tomorrow night?
Midnight @ the corner of Pine and 17th st.

I need you.

J.D.

whispers

On my own, she thought, creeping through the darkness.

It should have been terrifying — she was lost and alone, shivering in the wind and wandering aimlessly through deserted streets with unfamiliar names. The train station was only a mile from her house, but she'd been walking for almost an hour, which meant she must have made a wrong turn. Or several. She had no map, no phone, no way of finding her way forward or back — and no one to rescue her.

She should have been scared. She should have been trembling, crying, curled up in a ball, and waiting for help to arrive.

Instead, she was exhilarated.

She was free — free to make her own choices,

free from expectation, free from all the pressure bearing down on her, forcing her to be someone else. Someone normal.

And although she knew that if she didn't find the station soon, she would miss her train — would miss Daniel — she couldn't bring herself to worry. Somehow, after all that had gone wrong, she knew this would go right.

The station appeared two blocks later, just as the train chugged toward the platform. J.D. ran.

She raced through the small, heated station where a scattering of passengers waited, safe from the cold, stormed down the stairs to the platform, and threw herself into the train car just as the doors squeezed shut.

Then the train jolted into motion, and she was on her way.

J.D. paid the conductor with the bills she had slipped out of her mother's wallet — now she was a lunatic, a runaway, *and* a thief — and fell into a seat. She brushed away an abandoned newspaper and kicked at the empty plastic bottle at her feet, trying to catch her breath. She was moving.

Home — *Alexa's* home — was behind her, speeding

away into the distance. For a moment, she felt tempted to stay on the train forever, to go as far as it would take her, and never look back. She could leave it all behind. After all, what was there to go back to?

Dr. Styron's treatments?

A mental institution?

Nightmares?

Her mother.

Somehow, knowing that she had a choice — that she had *power* — made all the difference. She didn't have to go back, but she would. After she saw Daniel. After they figured things out together.

According to the schedule, the train ride would take forty minutes. She peered out the window, but all she could see was her own reflection. And the reflection of the man across the aisle.

He was staring at her.

J.D. forced herself not to turn around. When she'd gotten on the car, it had been empty. There was just her and the conductor. But now there was this man, this scowling, scruffy, glassy-eyed man. Watching her.

J.D. slumped down in her seat and pulled her scarf up over her chin. Of course. She should have realized that people would notice her, would recognize her face from their TV screens. She just hoped nobody would stop her, call her mother, send her home again. She had to blend in or she would miss her chance to see Daniel. Maybe her only chance.

She leaned her head back against the seat and closed her eyes.

Relax. Breathe in, breathe out, she told herself, just as Dr. Styron always did when he began their sessions together. *Relax your arms. Relax your legs. Calm. Peace. Relax.*

When she opened her eyes again, the man was gone.

The alley was narrow, crumbling, and smelled like garbage. In the dim orange glow from the flickering streetlight, J.D. could see the outline of her hand in front of her face but little else. So when the figure stepped out from the shadows, she almost screamed.

Then she did scream and ran toward him, throwing her arms around him and squeezing tight. Waiting in the dark, listening to the rats scrabbling through the piles of trash and the sirens in the distance, she had begun to wonder whether Daniel was just another phantom of her imagination. But now he was here. *Real.*

"Can't . . . breathe," he gasped, and she let go.

"Sorry." She stepped backward, suddenly embarrassed.

"No problem." He grinned. "I just didn't see that coming."

"Yeah. I . . . it's good to see you." J.D. didn't know what to say or where to look. In that first moment, she had felt such a flood of relief, like everything was going to be okay. But now?

She stared at the ground, at his scuffed sneakers. The laces on his left shoe were untied. She had only known him for a couple days, she realized. Yes, he was her only friend — the only person besides her mother she could ever remember trusting. But — for him — she was probably just some weird girl he'd met. Nothing special. She was lucky he'd shown up at all — but it was probably just to tell her that she should stop bothering him. And before he could get the words out, she had totally freaked him out.

"J.D.?" Daniel prompted. "What's going on? What's the big emergency?"

But she couldn't say anything. She stood there, head bowed, trying to decide what to do.

Then she opened her mouth, intending to apologize for dragging him out in the middle of the night — to tell him that he didn't have to feel obligated to her. That she didn't need him. Instead, it all came rushing to the surface. All the fear and frustration and anger she'd been holding down, day after day, trying to fit into her old life. All the messy emotions she'd tried her best to wall away came blasting through. She burst into tears.

And this time, he was the one who put his arms around her.

"We're *never* going to mention that again, okay?" J.D. managed a half smile, wiping away the last of her tears. It felt like it had taken forever, but she had finally cried herself out.

"What? The fact that you cried like a little baby?" Daniel grinned.

She slugged him lightly on the arm. The awkwardness between them had washed away.

"Ow!" he complained, rubbing his arm. "That's going to leave a bruise."

"Now who's the crybaby?"

"Still you, last time I checked," he said.

She brandished a fist. "What was that about bruising?" she joked.

He put up his arms. "I give, you win." He shook his head. "I forgot — you're dangerous."

His tone was light, but the words were enough to darken the mood.

"Thank you," she said quietly. "For coming, and for . . ."

"It's forgotten," he promised. "Really."

They stared at each other in silence again, but this time it wasn't awkward.

"Do you want to get out of here?" Daniel finally asked, nodding at the corroded brick walls and overflowing Dumpsters. "We could go get some coffee or something."

J.D. shook her head. She couldn't risk getting caught — and neither could he. Besides, the last train out of the city would be leaving soon, and she needed to be on it. "I don't have that much time," she said. "Can we just hang out here?"

"On one condition."

"What?"

"You tell me what's really going on with you," Daniel said. "You tell me everything."

So she did, beginning with the first time she'd met her mother. She told him about the sessions with Dr. Styron and the way she sometimes felt like he was her greatest enemy but other times, like he was the only one out there who could help her — the only one who wanted to.

"He's not," Daniel said firmly. It was the only time he interrupted.

She described her house and her bedroom and told him all about Alexa — how she was beginning to remember things she had done but not how it had felt to *be* Alexa, to live that carefree, happy life, to be unafraid. She told him about the nightmares and the visions and about her mother. "Every once in a while, she says something, or she looks at me in this certain way, and it's like she's not seeing Alexa, she's seeing *me*. The way I am now, you know? And I can tell that she loves me, even if I'm not . . ." J.D. was afraid she might start to tear up again, but she swallowed hard and forced the feeling away. "I guess I want to get better for her, as much as I do for me."

"Why?" Daniel asked.

"Because . . ." She hadn't stopped to think about it before, but now that she did, she realized that in the midst of all the confusion and suspicion, one thing made sense. "She's my mother. I love her." It was the first time she had admitted it out loud — or at all.

Daniel looked over her shoulder at something in the distance, his lips curled into a sad smile. "Then you're lucky."

"Maybe. But . . ." J.D. took a deep breath. "They want to send me away. To this, this Institute."

"What kind of institute?" he asked suspiciously.

"Kind of like a mental institution," J.D. admitted. "I saw this brochure, and it didn't look so bad. . . ."

"You sound like you're trying to talk yourself into it."

She shrugged, like it was no big deal. "What choice do I have? If I don't get better, they're going to force me to go. And if there's really something wrong with me, then maybe . . ."

"Maybe there's more Alexa in you than you think," Daniel said in disgust.

"What's that supposed to mean?"

"What choice do you have?" he repeated. "How about: *Don't go.* Don't let them convince you that you're crazy. You're *not*."

"I see things . . ." she whispered. "You don't know how bad it is sometimes. It's just . . ."

"So what? So you just give up? You let them send you off to the loony bin instead of figuring out what's going on? What if you're right, and this Styron guy really is up to something shady? You saw it, right?"

"You believe me?" J.D. asked.

"That shouldn't matter," Daniel said. "If you believe yourself, then what's the difference what anyone else thinks? Letting other people tell you what's real? *That's* crazy!" He paused. "But yeah. I believe you. Something's not right. He's trying to mess with your mind, turn you against yourself. I don't like it."

"So how do I fight back?"

"You could run," Daniel said. "I could go with you. We could leave tonight — get out and never come back."

And even though she'd had the idea herself only a couple hours before, it no longer appealed to her. "No. Not now, when I'm finally starting to remember. I can't run away. I won't let anyone drive me away from my home."

"So you stay."

"And get some answers," she said.

"We should start with Styron," Daniel suggested. "It all seems to go back to him. He's got you all turned around thinking you're losing it, he's turning your mother against you, he's messing with your mind. We've got to figure out what his agenda is. Can you get a look at his files or anything, snoop around his office?"

J.D. shook her head. "The only room I've ever been in doesn't have anything but a desk, a couch, and some chairs. No files, no —" She stopped abruptly, remembering.

"What?"

"There's another room, some kind of back office. That's where he keeps his computer."

"Great! Can you get in?"

She shook her head again. "No way. He never leaves me alone in there."

"So I'll do it," Daniel said. "I'll sneak out another night, break into the office, and —"

"No!" She couldn't let Daniel get in trouble for her. This was her battle, not his.

He pulled his lock-pick set out of his pocket. "Not a problem, remember? I can get in anywhere."

"Not there," she told him. "There's a serious alarm.

167

I've seen him turn it on at night. There's like six different codes. You'd never be able to get past it."

"So you can't get into his office. And I can't get into his office." Daniel narrowed his eyes. "But maybe together . . ."

"What are you thinking?"

"What if, during your session, there was some kind of emergency and Styron had to go take care of it —"

"Leaving me alone —"

"And giving you just enough time to figure out exactly what's going on."

"Could that really work?" J.D. asked.

"When's your next session?"

Having a plan made everything seem brighter. They stood under the flickering streetlight to say good-bye.

"I'll see you soon," Daniel promised.

"Thanks again," J.D. said. "I really —" She stopped, snapping her gaze toward the alley. She was sure she'd seen something move. Now — were those *eyes*, glinting in the dark?

"What?" Daniel asked.

"Shhh."

It could have been the wind. Or it could have been a whisper. *"J.D. . . ."*

"Did you hear that?" she asked.

Daniel cocked his head. "What?"

J.D. shrugged. "Probably nothing. It just sounded like —"

The man rushed out of the darkness and hurtled into Daniel, knocking him against the side of a building. He slumped to the ground.

"Daniel!" she shrieked, but then the man was on her, his dirty fingers wrapped around her wrists, dragging her back toward the alley. "No!" She screamed and struggled and kicked wildly, as hard as she could, her foot connecting with something soft. He grunted and, as his grasp slipped, she ran.

Two heavy footsteps behind her, then he was on her again, trapping her in a corner. "Calm down, J.D.," he said, reaching for something in his pocket. "I'm here to help."

She flailed wildly, but he lunged at her, and in his hand he had a handkerchief, and he was bringing it toward her nose and mouth. She breathed in the chemical fumes and almost choked, then jerked her head away and took a deep, gasping breath of fresh air. But he shoved the cloth against her again, slamming her head back against the wall. She tried to hold her breath.

Had he said her name?

She had to breathe. The handkerchief was wet with something. The scent was almost sweet. She couldn't escape it. Couldn't escape him.

The world was getting blurry, dizzy. Everything seemed to be moving very slowly.

"That's right," he murmured. "Just a little more. Breathe in, breathe out . . ."

And it was so easy, just like on the couch in Dr. Styron's office, soft and cozy, her head pressed against the pillow, her eyes closed, everything calm. Peaceful. Safe. So easy . . .

No!

Her eyes shot open, and she reached for his neck, without thinking, just desperate. She blinked rapidly, trying to hold her breath and keep her head clear, trying to reach his throat, her fingers hot, tingling, squeezing, wishing —

And then, though she hadn't touched him, he gasped.

His grip loosened. The handkerchief fell to the ground.

J.D. breathed.

Her attacker didn't.

His eyes bugged out. His hands clawed at his throat. His face turned pale. His lips moved. *Please.* No sound came out.

"J.D.!"

She jerked her head toward the sound of Daniel's voice — and the man let out a long, rasping sigh. She turned back to him quickly enough to see the look in his eyes.

Terror.

And then he ran.

"J.D! Are you okay?" Daniel picked himself up and, rubbing the back of his head where it had smashed into the brick, hurried over to her. "Did he hurt you?"

She pressed her hand lightly against her neck. She could almost still feel his dirty fingers around her throat. And yet — he hadn't hurt her. She had hurt him.

Somehow.

She took a step toward Daniel, then staggered, still dizzy from whatever the man had tried to poison her with. Everything was swimming in front of her, and nothing made sense. Daniel grabbed her arm and lowered her to the ground. They sat together, backs against the wall, shoulders touching.

"How did you get away?" Daniel finally asked.

"I don't know," she said. Everything had happened so fast. She could remember trying to strangle him, but she hadn't been able to reach — or had she?

"Okay," Daniel said quietly, in a calming voice. "It's going to be okay."

"I think . . . I think he knew me," J.D. whispered. "I think he said my name."

"But — that doesn't make any sense. Are you sure?"

"Maybe. No. I don't know."

"Maybe he was watching us," Daniel guessed. "He could have heard me say your name."

"But why would he be watching us?" she asked, thinking, *Why would he be watching me?* She suddenly remembered the guy on the train. Was it the same man? It could have been.

It could have been anyone.

"It was just some crazy guy," Daniel said, sounding sure. "Probably high on something, wanted money. He wasn't after you. It was just bad luck. We were in the wrong place at the wrong time. Don't let yourself think it's anything more than that."

Don't be paranoid. She knew that's what he really meant, he just didn't want to say it.

This wasn't paranoia. Someone had attacked her. That wasn't her imagination. And the way the man had stared at her — he *had* known her. She was certain of it.

away

"Time to get up, hon!" There were three loud raps on the door. "Sweetie? Are you awake?"

J.D. moaned and pulled the covers over her head. "Five more minutes," she mumbled. She turned over onto her back and stretched out across the bed, trying to wake herself up. She didn't want to be late for school —

She stopped herself. School?

For a moment, she had felt normal again. Like a sleepy eighth grader who stayed up too late watching TV. Like Alexa.

But she hadn't been watching TV. She had been sneaking through the slumbering city, fighting off attackers, walking the chilly mile home from the train station, slipping into the house just before three AM.

"Are you hungry?" her mother asked from outside

174

the door. "I have a little surprise for you down-stairs."

"I'll be down in a minute!" J.D. called. She sat up in bed and rubbed her eyes. Her memories of the night before seemed flimsy, like they belonged to a different world. They didn't belong here, in her safe, frilly bedroom, under her cozy, pink comforter. They felt like they belonged to a different life.

And this *is the life I want*, she told herself.

She padded downstairs in her pajamas, trying to decide whether to tell her mother about sneaking out of the house. It would surely get her in trouble, and mess up her plan with Daniel. But J.D. just couldn't forget the attack. What if the man came after her again? What if he found her here, at home?

"Chocolate-chip pancakes," her mother said, holding up a bright yellow bowl filled with batter.

"The Sunday Special!" J.D. said eagerly, hurrying to join her at the counter.

Her mother looked thrilled. "You remember Sunday Specials?"

J.D. nodded, realizing that she did. "Something about . . . Mickey Mouse?" she asked doubtfully, trying to make sense of the images floating through her mind.

"When you were little, I used to make you Sunday pancakes in the shape of Mickey's head," her mother explained. "We still did it — do it, I mean — these days. For special occasions."

"Is today a special occasion?"

Her mother leaned over and gave her a soft kiss on the cheek. "You're home. You're safe. And you remember my pancakes. That's special enough for me." She handed J.D. a spoon and, feeling like she'd done it a million times before, J.D. began to stir.

"So, did you sleep well last night?" her mother asked.

J.D. nodded, swooshing the batter around in the bowl. She felt bad lying, but what was she supposed to do?

"The reason I ask is, well . . ."

J.D. tensed — there was something off about her mother's tone. Did she know that J.D. had snuck out of the house? Could she know why? Frantic, she tried to come up with some kind of excuse, some way to explain herself. But maybe this was a sign. Maybe it was finally time to tell the truth.

"I heard you last night," her mother continued, sounding almost apologetic. "Screaming."

J.D. whirled around. "*What?*"

Her mother sat down at the kitchen table and began rubbing the back of her neck. "I don't want to pressure you, darling, but if the nightmares are getting this bad, maybe it's time we talk about them."

J.D. had barely slept at all last night — she'd only been in bed for an hour or two. "I don't, uh, remember having any bad dreams," she said, hoping she sounded casual.

"Really?" Her mother frowned. "You were tossing and turning all night — I woke up the first time you screamed and then . . ." Her cheeks turned a pale pink. "I didn't want to wake you up, since you need your sleep, but . . . I know this sounds overprotective, but I checked on you every hour or so, just to make sure you were all right."

"You checked on me *every hour*?" J.D. asked incredulously.

Her mother laughed softly. "I know it seems silly, but I'm your mother. I worry. It's part of the job description. And I wouldn't have been able to sleep anyway, not with you down the hall, having such terrible dreams."

J.D. gasped and staggered back against the kitchen counter. The bowl of batter fell from her hands and clattered against the tile floor. She barely even noticed. If her mother had checked on her every hour . . . if she'd been in bed all night . . .

She shook her head. "No," she whispered, feeling like a hand was tightening around her throat. "It's not possible." She could remember it all so clearly. She could almost *see* it — the train ride. The alley. The attack. Daniel. It was all real, as real as anything that had ever happened to her. So how could it have been her imagination?

You could retreat into a world of delusion, Dr. Styron had warned. *Lose touch with reality.*

She had so few memories — how many of them were real? And how many were lies she'd told herself, hallucinations so vivid she had mistaken them for truth?

"J.D.?" her mother asked in concern, rising from the chair.

If she couldn't trust herself, how was she supposed to know *what* was real? For all she knew, she could be dreaming right now. For all she knew, Daniel himself was a fantasy.

"No," she moaned. Not possible — not her only friend, the one person she could count on.

But isn't that oh-so-convenient? a cynical voice in her head asked. *Your loyal ally against the rest of the world, willing to do anything for you, even though he's only known you a few days. Isn't it all a little . . . too good to be true?*

"No!" she cried again.

The next thing she knew, her mother had grabbed her by the shoulders and was shaking her roughly. "J.D.!" she shouted. "Snap out of it."

I checked on you every hour.

J.D. burst into tears, throwing her arms around her mother and squeezing as tight as she could. There was no escaping reality anymore, no denying the truth.

She was losing her mind.

And she needed help.

"J.D., honey, what is it?" her mother asked, rubbing J.D.'s back in slow circles. Her hands were warm. But for a long time, J.D. couldn't speak. She just sobbed, holding tight to her mother, to the one thing she knew was real. Finally, she ran out of tears.

Her mother led her over to a chair. J.D. sat down carefully, feeling shaky and fragile, like every inch of her skin was bruised and even the slightest touch would hurt. Her mother sat down next to her and reached for J.D.'s hand. She gave it a quick squeeze.

"J.D., you're scaring me. What's going on?"

J.D. took a deep breath. She was scared, too. Every

time she closed her eyes to blink, she was afraid she would open them on a different reality. How had she let things get so bad? Or — and this was almost too terrifying to think — had they been this bad all along? So much had happened to her since that day she woke up in the rubble. How much of it had been a deluded fantasy?

"Don't be mad, but there's some stuff I haven't told you," she finally admitted in a soft voice just above a whisper.

"I'm not mad. But honey, you know you can tell me anything."

"I know. And I want to. But it's going to sound . . ." *Just spit it out*, she told herself. She couldn't handle this on her own. Not anymore. "Sometimes I see things, and, uh, hear music — or voices. Hallucinations, I guess. Just like Dr. Styron said. And sometimes I feel like I can . . . do stuff. Stuff that doesn't make sense."

A strange expression flashed across her mother's face — it was almost a smile. But it was gone almost as quickly as it had appeared. And J.D. knew she must have imagined it, just like everything else.

"I'll be standing there talking to someone, and then, whoosh, I'm somewhere else," J.D. confessed. It felt good to say it out loud. It felt good to finally tell the truth. "It's like I'm in the middle of this horrible nightmare all the time, and I can act normal, and sometimes it even seems like things *are* normal, and then suddenly I'm back in the nightmare all over again and —" She hugged her mother, pressing her face into her mother's shoulder. "I just want to wake up. Please. I'll do anything. Just . . . help me."

Her mother's hand smoothed down her hair. "It'll be okay," she promised. "I'll take care of everything."

There wasn't much to pack.

"The Institute will have everything you need," her mother had assured her. "And I can bring up more of your things later on, once we see . . . once we decide how long you'll need to be there."

They would go to Dr. Styron's office first. J.D. would finally tell him the truth about everything that had been happening to her. She was looking forward to this part most of all, because she needed to know the truth.

Her mother could pretend everything was going to be okay — but Dr. Styron was a doctor. J.D. knew that if she pressed him, he would be honest about her condition. He would tell her whether she could ever be normal again.

Packing went quickly. She grabbed a couple T-shirts, an old pair of jeans. Would she wear normal clothes in the Institute, or would there be some kind of uniform? Or maybe a hospital gown?

She forced herself to stop wondering. She just had to get through the next few hours, moment by moment, without thinking about what came next.

She opened a drawer to discover the worn green pajamas she'd worn at the Center for Juvenile Services. She pulled them out — it would be comforting to have them with her at the Institute, some reminder of the past.

Then she thought better of it and threw them down on her bed. *J.D. isn't real*, Dr. Styron lectured in her head. *The tighter you hold on to this new self, the more fractured your identity becomes.*

She reached up to touch the silver lock picks hanging around her neck — they were her last and best connection to Daniel, to the Center, to all the moments that had made her J.D. She had promised herself she would never take them off. But . . .

The Greenborough Institute was her last resort. If it didn't work, she would have no options left. Which meant she had to try — *really* try — to do things right. Even when it hurt.

She unhooked the chain and placed it on top of her bureau. Then she opened her sock drawer and pulled out the small jewelry box her mother had given her. The delicate silver heart was even more beautiful than she'd remembered. J.D. slipped the lock picks off the chain and threaded it back through the heart, then laced the pendant around her neck.

She was ready to be Alexa.

She was ready to say good-bye.

locked

My name is Alexa, she told herself, walking into Dr. Styron's office. *I'll do whatever I have to do.*

"Alexa," he said, giving her an approving smile. "You've made the right choice. I'm certain the Greenborough Institute will be the answer."

She took a seat in one of his hard-backed chairs. This wasn't a couch kind of day.

"What will they do to me there? How will they fix me?" J.D. didn't yet dare ask the question she had really come to ask. *What happens if even* they *can't fix me? Where do I go then?*

"I will oversee your treatment myself," Dr. Styron explained. "We will continue the hypnotherapy, since you've shown some promising progress with that course of treatment. But the frequency and intensity of the sessions will, of course, increase.

And we'll also start you on a drug protocol designed to chemically unlock the doors to your past."

J.D. pictured herself as a drugged-up zombie, wandering the halls blindly, trapped forever inside her nightmares. But she forced the image out of her head. Dr. Styron wouldn't send her off to a fate like that.

Her mother would never let it happen.

"What if that doesn't work?" she asked softly.

He smiled. "I don't want you to worry, Alexa. But I will be honest. If it doesn't work, you will retreat further and further from reality. And you will almost surely become a danger to others and to yourself. But by then, I'm afraid, it would be too late to repair the damage."

J.D. was trembling. *A danger to others and to yourself.* She remembered the sound of Mel's head hitting the concrete, remembered staring at Daniel, a shard of glass clenched in her fist.

She was already dangerous. She was already out of control.

She pressed her lips together, refusing to cry.

Dr. Styron stood up and took a step toward her, but before he could take another, the intercom on his desk buzzed.

"I told you I wasn't to be interrupted!" he snapped into it.

"I'm sorry," the receptionist's voice blared. "But it's an emergency. There's a boy out here, he's having some kind of seizure — I don't know what, but it's bad, we need you!" J.D. could hear a boy's shouts and cries through the intercom — the voice sounded familiar.

Dr. Styron grunted and rolled his eyes — but then, quickly, the familiar expression of gentle concern returned to his face. "I'm very sorry," he told J.D., patting her on the shoulder. "I'll be back as soon as I can."

She nodded, thinking only: *Daniel!*

He'd come to save her.

If Daniel was here, that meant last night had happened. She had gone into the city and they had come up with a plan together. It meant that her memories were real.

But her mother had seen her in bed every hour, tossing and turning in her sleep. Or so her mother had said. Which meant that the boy having a seizure outside — the distraction that had conveniently left her alone in Dr. Styron's office, free to do whatever she wanted — was either a bizarre coincidence, or . . . her mother was lying.

It was an option J.D. didn't even want to consider. The idea that her mother would let her believe she'd gone crazy — that her mother had watched her break down into uncontrollable sobs and *still* kept up the lie — it was too much to handle. So J.D. didn't think. She moved. If Daniel was here, it meant he was giving her one last chance to find out the truth. And it was a chance she had to take.

The hall was deserted. There was only one other door on the long corridor — Dr. Styron's private office. J.D. put her hand on the knob and paused, feeling her body pulse with fear.

She twisted the knob. But the door was locked. J.D.'s hand flew to her neck, to grab Daniel's lock picks — and then she remembered. The picks were in her bureau at home. All she had now was a silver heart. Useless.

A silver heart — and two bobby pins holding her hair back from her face. Maybe not so useless after all.

The pins weren't as fancy as Daniel's specially made tools, but maybe they would work. She inserted one in the lock, to use it as a tension wrench, then began jiggling the other one around, feeling for the tumblers. But the pins were too small and kept slipping out of her fingers, and she couldn't trip the second pin without losing the first one, and she was running out of time, and . . .

Just open, she thought furiously, jamming the pins in almost at random now, desperate to get inside before she lost her chance. She banged her forehead against the door with a soft thud. Her whole life had been reduced to a series of locked doors, inside her mind and now out. She needed to break through, just once. Was that so much to —

She felt the telltale click of the lock, and the door swung open. She stuffed the pins into her pocket and stepped inside, easing the door shut behind her.

It wasn't an office or a records room, or any kind of room at all. It was just an oversized storage area, completely bare, except for a table shoved up against the wall. A table with a laptop on it.

She flipped open the computer and the screen flickered to life. There were five icons on the desktop; she chose the miniature camera and an empty screen clicked open, with a variety of files to choose from. There were no names attached, only dates and times. J.D. chose at random. And pressed play.

The video was just like the one she'd seen before. The screen version of J.D. lay on the couch as Dr. Styron spoke the familiar, soothing words. Glancing nervously at the clock, J.D. hit the fast forward button, and watched herself fall quickly asleep. She had intended to hit play again midway through the session, when the hypnosis would be deep enough that she would start talking about her memories. But then it happened.

Dr. Styron went over to his desk and pulled something out of the drawer. He walked back to the couch, and J.D. leaned closer to the screen, trying to figure out what he held in his hand. He bent over her sleeping body and raised his arm.

J.D. gasped. He was holding a needle. A long, thick syringe filled with a pale green liquid. "No," she whispered, but on the screen, she slept. Dr. Styron smiled. And then he injected her, jamming the needle into her arm and pressing down on the syringe. The green liquid slowly seeped into her body.

And the J.D. on screen began to scream.

"I know it hurts," Dr. Styron said calmly. "Ignore the pain."

The screaming stopped.

"Sit up," he said. The J.D. on screen followed his

command. Her mouth stretched into an eerie smile that matched his.

Dr. Styron sat down across from her and spoke in a low, soothing voice. "It's Christmas. You smell the gingerbread. Your mother laughs. You love the sound of your mother's laugh, almost as much as you love gingerbread cookies."

"I love the sound of my mother's laugh," the on-screen J.D. repeated, her voice flat and toneless. "Almost as much as I love gingerbread cookies."

"There are presents under the tree," Dr. Styron continued. "You are not allowed to open them."

"I am not allowed to open them," J.D. said robotically.

J.D. was shaking. Her hands grabbed the edge of the table, turning white as she clenched down, trying to keep herself from crying out. But the J.D. on screen just sat quietly, smiling that placid, creepy smile and talking in that flat, robotic voice.

"Your name is Alexa." Dr. Styron held up a photograph. "And this is your mother."

"My name is Alexa. And that is my mother."

"And you love her very much," Dr. Styron said.

"And I love her very much."

J.D. was so focused on the computer screen that

she didn't hear the door open. "I'm sorry you had to see that," the voice in the doorway said. "But it makes this easier."

When J.D. finally turned, all she saw was the mouth of the gun.

Strangely, she felt no fear. Even after the gunshot. And the pain.

Only as she was falling out of the chair — and it felt like it was happening so slowly, like she was floating to the ground — only when she was lying on the floor, the darkness creeping into her field of vision, the footsteps drawing closer, and she was unable to move, unable to scream, unable to breathe, only then did she feel afraid.

And it only lasted a moment.

Then she felt nothing at all.

lies

She opened her eyes.

Alive, she thought.

She struggled to sit up. Couldn't. She lay on her side, her arms pinned flat across her chest. Her head throbbed, especially when she tried to move. But she moved anyway, pressing her chin against her chest to get a better look at herself — to check for a wound.

There was no blood.

She had been wearing a dark green sweater with a pale blue stripe along the collar. But when she looked down now, she saw a featureless white jacket. The material was coarse and heavy. Her arms were crossed, like she was hugging herself, and pressed so tightly against her chest that she had trouble breathing.

The word floated to the top of her mind: *straitjacket*.

Along with the word, images, maybe from an old

movie: wild-eyed, raving lunatics, shrieking nonsense into the darkness. Mad scientists. Electro-shock. Padded walls.

And straitjackets.

J.D. tried to stay calm. Focus. She needed to escape. But first, she needed to think. She was lying on her side in a small, dark space. The floor was cold and hard. Her back was pressed up against something softer, almost padded. The ceiling was low — so low that she would have bumped her head against it if she had been able to stand. And in front of her — doors, two of them, like car doors, only taller. She was locked in the back of a van.

She struggled to free herself from the straitjacket, but it was wrapped too tight. And even if she could roll herself across the floor of the van, what good would it do? She couldn't open the doors, much less jump out. She couldn't even sit up.

Her head was foggy, and her thoughts kept slipping away from her. It was so hard to concentrate. But she had to come up with a plan. The van wasn't moving yet. But it would, soon. They were taking her somewhere — unless she'd slept through the journey and they had already arrived.

A door slammed. There was a rustling noise

behind her, where the driver's seat must be. She was no longer alone.

"I know you're awake."

J.D. closed her eyes and held herself very still.

"There's no use in pretending. A mother always knows."

"You're not my mother," J.D. spat out.

"You have to believe me," the woman who wasn't her mother said calmly. "I can help you. I know it must seem like —"

"*Help me?*" Even through her terror and panic, J.D. managed to choke out a bitter laugh. "You *shot* me. You tied me up and threw me in the back of a van. You've been lying to me this whole time, trying to convince me I'm someone I'm not, trying to convince me I'm crazy. Is that your way of helping?"

"It was just a tranquilizer gun."

"Oh, that's *so* much better."

"J.D., it's complicated. I didn't want it to happen like this, but it's the only way we could be together."

I loved her, J.D. thought, hating herself for being so stupid, for believing the lies. *She was my mother.*

But she wasn't. J.D. understood that now. She didn't understand anything else that was going on, but she got that much. She had no mother. No home. Only a head full of lies.

"I can't explain things to you now," the woman said. "There's no time. But you have to trust me —"

"*Trust you?*"

"Honey . . ."

"Don't call me that," J.D. said coldly. She refused to reveal her pain. "Just admit it. Admit that it was all a lie."

"It was all a lie," the woman said flatly. "There is no Alexa Collins. The house was a fake. The pictures were faked. The memories were faked. The whole thing was an elaborate fiction, to keep your mind under control. Congratulations, you're officially too smart for your own good."

Even though she'd already figured out those truths, J.D. felt like she'd been kicked in the stomach. To hear it out loud . . . to hear that everything she'd believed in and everything she'd been told about herself was a lie . . . It meant she was right back at the beginning, a stranger to herself.

And she was terrified. Because now that the charade was up, what were they going to do to her?

"Why?" J.D. asked. "Why did you do this? What do you want from me?"

"You're too dangerous — if you were to get out of control . . . I needed you to trust me."

"You want me to trust you, how about we lose the straitjacket?" J.D. said, trying to sound tough.

The woman laughed — and it wasn't the soft, melodic laugh that J.D. had come to know over the last several days. It was harsh now and without joy. "Nice try. But you're staying back there for now. It's for your own good. And mine, for that matter. You have no idea how dangerous you are. Getting you out of the way will make things safer for everyone."

Out of the way.

Permanently?

J.D. didn't feel dangerous. She felt like her time was running out.

"Enough of this," the woman said irritably. "Everything's taken care of, and now we have to get going. I wish I could say I'll explain everything on the drive, but I'm afraid I just can't take that risk."

"What risk?"

"The risk of having you awake," the woman said. "That dosage normally puts people out for at least an hour — but when have you ever been normal? I can see you're going to need something stronger." A door slammed, and after a moment of silence, the door to J.D.'s compartment flew open. Light streamed inside. Her mother raised the gun. "I could tell you this isn't going to hurt, but I think we're both tired of the lies, don't you?"

J.D. refused to plead with her or look away. She just stared the woman in the face, daring her to shoot.

But as her finger squeezed down on the trigger, there was a howl of rage and a small body slammed into her from behind, knocking the gun out of her hands. The shot went wild as the woman tumbled forward into the van, knocking her head against the floor.

"J.D., come on, let's go!" It was Daniel, and before she knew what was happening, he had grabbed her shoulder and tugged her out of the van and onto her feet. His fingers fumbled with the latches on the straitjacket and then suddenly she was free.

"How did you — where —?" she stammered, as they raced across the empty parking lot. She could hear the woman chasing after them and didn't dare to look back.

"Tell you later," Daniel panted. "Just run."

...y more breath. They ran faster, ...cking off the street and cutting across lawns, through backyards, darting around corners.

J.D. felt like her lungs would burst, but she ran faster still. Her feet pounded the pavement. Daniel fell behind for a moment, then pulled even with her again. Behind them, the woman was shouting something, her words lost on the wind. J.D. didn't care. Nothing the woman had to say could matter to her anymore. She just needed to get away.

She heard only her own breath whistling through her lungs. She stumbled and almost fell, but Daniel grabbed her and pulled her up. She didn't have enough breath to thank him, and there was no time.

"In there!" Daniel rasped, pointing ahead of them.

"The train station?" J.D. shook her head. The building was too small. There was nowhere to hide, and when the woman found them, they'd be cornered. Trapped.

"No, *there*."

To one side of the station, there was a small, empty field. But on the other side, there was a crumbling building that looked like it had once been a farmhouse. Now it was just a wreck.

They burst through the doors of the train station

and pushed through the small crowd, then escaped out a side exit, and took off for the abandoned building. Daniel headed for the door, but J.D. stopped him.

"Windows," she hissed. They rounded the back of the building. Three wide-pane windows stood at floor level. Daniel kicked in the glass and ducked inside, then guided J.D. through the shards.

Hopefully, the woman would think they'd taken refuge in the train station — it could buy them a few minutes while she searched.

"We should keep going," Daniel urged her. "She'll find us here."

"We can't keep running forever," J.D. said. "But maybe we can find a good place to hide."

They found a staircase that creaked with every step. On the second floor, as below, there were no rooms, no doors, only a wide, open landing with a thick wooden banister at the edge. But on one end, there was a small alcove stuffed with empty boxes. J.D. and Daniel climbed inside and piled the boxes in front of them, forming a cardboard wall.

It was too dark to see anything, but their shoulders were pressed together. J.D. liked it that way — it gave her proof that he was there.

"How did you find me?" she whispered.

"I faked a seizure, and they carried me outside," he whispered back. "I ran away. Then I watched. And eventually, I saw her carry you out to the van. Is that . . . was she your mother?"

"No." J.D. closed her eyes for a moment. "I mean, I thought she . . . but no. She's not."

"So I guess this makes us even."

"For what?"

"You rescued me, and now I rescued you," he pointed out. "Even."

"Hey, I rescued myself," she protested. "You just gave me the opening."

"Whatever you need to tell yourself," he teased. "*I* know the truth. I'm like a superhero."

"You're *like* an egomaniac." She squeezed his hand, then quickly let go. "But thank you."

Neither of them spoke. And then the sound of breaking glass punctured the silence.

"I know you're in here!" the woman shouted.

J.D. held very still and very silent and waited for the end.

lost

They could hear her footsteps padding back and forth across the ground floor, searching.

"This isn't what you think!" the woman shouted from below. Her voice echoed through the empty building. "I'm not with them. If you'd just come out, I can help you."

Let her talk, J.D. thought. *Let her scream and yell, let her make a thousand promises.* J.D. would never believe her. Not after the lies.

Something was bubbling through her, an emotion so fierce it made her shake. At first, drawing in long, silent breaths through a clenched jaw, she thought it was terror. But there was something else, something louder than the fear. Anger.

No, rage.

This woman and Dr. Styron had tried to steal her from herself. They had tried to tear down her personality, piece by piece, replace it with a fantasy of their own — and then convince her that *she* was the crazy one. For all she knew, they were the ones behind her memory loss in the first place, the ones responsible for this nightmare she'd been drowning in. She'd thought they were trying to pull her to safety, when all the while they'd had their hands pressed against her head, pushing her under.

I never loved her, J.D. told herself. *Not really. Deep down, a part of me must have sensed the truth.*

But that was just another lie.

She was tired of running, tired of hiding. She wanted answers. She wanted to fight. She tensed, drawing her strength together, preparing to jump out and reveal herself. But as if he knew, Daniel's grip bore down on her arm.

"No," he whispered, almost inaudibly. "Wait."

If she had been alone, it wouldn't have mattered. She didn't care what happened to her next. She just wanted revenge; she wanted it to be over. But she wasn't alone. And somehow she knew that while they — whoever *they* were — needed something from her, they didn't need Daniel. He was expendable.

The stairs began to creak. She was getting closer.

J.D. peered through a gap in the boxes, needing

to know what was coming, and when. The woman crept along the landing, her heels clicking with every step. She was carrying a long, crooked wooden plank with a fiery tip. It lit her way through the darkness, casting flickering shadows through the crumbling ruin of a house.

She paused before the alcove, peering at the stack of boxes, then raised the tranquilizer gun. And for a moment, J.D. was sure their eyes had met. The flame gave the woman's face a reddish–orange cast. Her long blond hair was tangled, her clothes dirty. A purplish bruise spread across one side of her face.

"I don't want to hurt you," the woman said. "I just need you to come with me. You *are* coming with me. As for the boy . . . leave now, and you won't be hurt."

Daniel's fingers tightened on J.D.'s arm. He wasn't going anywhere.

The woman shook her head. "Stay, and I can't make you any promises." She took a step toward the alcove. "But J.D. is coming with me, one way or another."

It was too much. J.D. ripped her arm away from Daniel and lunged through the wall of boxes. "Leave me alone!" she shrieked. The woman backed away, her face twisted in terror.

They stood motionless, staring at each other, several feet of space between them. The woman's back was pressed up against the banister.

"Leave," J.D. said coolly, the fury rippling through her. There was something about the expression on the woman's face that made J.D. feel like she was the one with all the power. "Leave now."

"It's too dangerous," the woman said. She took a step toward J.D. "This is my responsibility, and I won't —"

"J.D., *run!*" Daniel burst into the open and grabbed J.D. The woman scowled, raised her gun, took aim, and —

"*Noooo!*" J.D. screamed as a rush of hot anger flooded through her body. She thrust her arms out toward the woman, knowing it was useless, there was no stopping her — but the gun never fired. The woman stumbled backward — no, *flew* backward — over the banister, then flailing, screaming all the way down until she landed at the bottom with a sickening thud.

And then she was silent.

Flames from her makeshift torch crawled across

the littered debris, jumping to the piles of empty boxes and soon climbing up the decaying walls.

The woman — the body — her mother — didn't move.

That wasn't my mother, J.D. told herself. She tried to remember the gun, the straitjacket, the cold, cruel smile.

But all she could think of was the warmth of her mother's embrace. Soft lips brushing her forehead. The smell of gingerbread.

"We have to get out of here," Daniel said in a shaky voice. J.D. couldn't look at him. She couldn't look at anything but the woman, surrounded by a ring of fire.

"J.D., *fire*. We have to *go*."

When she didn't speak, didn't move — because she *couldn't* — he grabbed her by the waist and pushed her ahead of him, across the landing, down the steps, seconds before the flames raced across the floor to consume them. Through the window and into the open air, their faces gray with soot, their lungs choked with smoke. She didn't want to stay and watch the building burn, but she couldn't bring herself to turn away, so again Daniel grabbed her, and again they ran. She imagined that the woman was still chasing them — but when she looked back, no one was there.

"I think we're safe now," Daniel said, once they'd put what felt like miles between them and the building. The fire. The body.

Safe? J.D. wanted to laugh but couldn't.

They stopped in an alley. And finally, she looked at Daniel. His eyes were wide, his face pale. And he was watching her.

"What did you do back there?" he whispered. "*How* did you do that?"

J.D. didn't answer. She just looked down at her hands. She hadn't touched the woman, she was sure of it. And yet . . . she could remember how it felt, pushing her mother back, releasing all that anger and frustration and fear in a single, deadly thrust.

Not my mother, she reminded herself furiously.

The woman's words repeated in her head. *You don't know how dangerous you are. You don't know how dangerous you are.* She wondered how long it would take the flames to consume the body. She wondered if it had hurt.

"*What did you do?*" Daniel asked again, louder this time. J.D. tried to touch his shoulder, but he jerked away.

"I don't know," she mumbled. It felt like a lie.

Who was she, really? *What* was she? She needed to know — now more than ever. Dr. Styron would come for her, she knew that. She would never be able to escape, not until she learned the truth about what she was running from. And the truth about herself.

It should have seemed hopeless — but somehow, it didn't. J.D. stared at her hands again, turning them over one by one.

They had said she was unstable, out of control. That she didn't know what she was capable of. They had said she was dangerous.

Maybe they were right.

Robin Wasserman remembers almost everything that ever happened to her. She remembers the names of all her teachers and where she sat in their classrooms. She remembers her first goldfish, her pink stuffed elephant, her nursery school nemesis, and the theme song of every TV show she's ever seen. Her friends find this odd. Her parents find it annoying, especially when she interrupts family dinners to say things like, "Remember fourth-grade Halloween when you made me cover up my pixie costume with an ugly brown coat? Why are you always trying to ruin my life?" But mostly, she remembers good things, which is why she's in no hurry to grow up.

Robin lives in New York City, where she writes books and sometimes rides her bike very fast through the park, pretending she's on a secret mission and being chased by the forces of evil.

As far as she knows, that's just her imagination.

chasing yesterday   #2 betrayal

robin wasserman

SCHOLASTIC

J.D. is on the run, searching for answers about her past . . . and about the strange and dangerous abilities she's beginning to discover she has. She knows she can't trust the memories implanted in her mind by the mysterious Dr. Styron, but they still feel real — and they won't stop haunting her. J.D. and Daniel must race to uncover the truth and unlock the dark secrets in her brain . . . before it's too late.

Hidden pasts.
Unexpected betrayals.
Twisted friendships.
Sweet revenge.

Don't miss

Little Secrets

by Emily Blake

Turn the page for a sneak peek at book one:

Playing with Fire

Let the drama begin . . .

Chapter 1

There were only two things Alison Rose knew she could count on: her best friend and cousin, Kelly, and the fact that everyone else in her family would stop at nothing to destroy one another.

Like now. Alison was in the middle of a battle with her made-of-steel mother. And this time she was not going to lose. Digging her orange-painted nails into her palms, she lobbed a verbal grenade.

"It's not like I expect you to come to anything I do," Alison said. After fifteen years she knew better than that. She took a breath and did her best to keep her voice steady. If she lost her temper, her mother would refuse to discuss it any further. Period. "But I can't miss this game," she said evenly. "It's the championship. The last game of the season. Besides, people are relying on me — I'm part of a team."

Halfway across the living room, Helen Rose sat

in the wingback chair wearing her sky-blue cash-mere bathrobe — the one that matched her eyes. Her short auburn hair was perfectly styled after a long day of work. It always was. After all, her illustrious career as a domestic trendsetter was based on being perfectly styled.

"Teams are for people who don't have the ability to get anywhere on their own," Helen replied. She did not bother to look up from her laptop. It was a tactic Alison knew she used on her employees when she wanted them to feel insignificant. But Helen underestimated her daughter: Alison was tougher than your usual CEO's assistant — and better trained.

"Or for people who know how to cooperate," Alison shot back smoothly.

Helen's eyes remained fixed on the computer screen, but Alison saw her face tighten. "I don't see why I should let you use the driver on Saturday when you're too busy to make an appearance with me on Sunday," she stated calmly. "After all, the book signing is a good opportunity for both of us." She checked her manicure and waited for Alison to comply like she usually did.

There was no way. Not this time. First of all,

Alison did not work for her mother. Second, she was not about to miss the championship game. And third, she was sick and tired of playing the happy daughter at her mother's endless string of events.

"If you are so anxious for us to look like a normal family, maybe you should try acting like a normal mother, *Honey*."

Alison knew her mother despised her real name, along with just about everything else Alison's grandmother Tamara Diamond had given her. Helen and Tamara had stopped speaking long ago — before Alison was born. Warm and fuzzy mother-daughter relations did not run in the Diamond family.

When Helen finally turned and looked Alison in the face, Alison could see the crow's feet around her light eyes. She'd landed a hit. The wound was open — time for the salt. "I'm already going to a 'family' event on Sunday anyway. Why don't you tell your fans and TV crews that I'm at Grandmother's? You haven't forgotten her birthday, have you?" Alison's fingers uncurled as she gained the upper hand. Her mother pretended not to be bothered, but Alison could tell by her flaring nostrils that she was . . . and that she was calculating her next move.

Alison braced herself. It wasn't like she enjoyed

this. What she wanted more than anything else was a normal life. A mother who cared about her. A father who bothered to show up. A family that got along . . . and didn't own half the town.

Helen was silent as she struggled behind her mask of calm. She didn't like to be reminded that she was the one who was too busy for Alison and not the other way around. More than that, she hated any reference to the Diamond/Rose family feud. The severed ties were a nasty blemish on Helen's otherwise perfect appearance. And Helen Rose cared about nothing more than appearances. She had, quite literally, written the book on it: *Helen Rose's Looking Good*. The book had made her a household name, along with her magazine and the hundreds of *Looking Good* household items available at a fine retailer near you.

She'd just love to stick me *on a shelf,* Alison thought. All too often she felt like one of her mother's products — stamped with Helen's name and her "busy" bumblebee emblem — made to "look good." But Alison knew there was a big difference between looking good and feeling good.

Breathing through her nose, Helen slid her reading glasses back on and peered once again at her laptop. She was finished arguing and was now doing what she called "getting busy." It was what she did whenever she didn't want to deal with something, especially her daughter.

Ding. Alison had won the round, even if she hadn't really managed to win her mother's attention.

"So, I can take the limo?" Alison drummed her fingernails on the marble mantel and watched her mother turn away, as if Alison were dragging her nails down a chalkboard. Alison knew she could have the car. She just wanted to hear Helen say it.

She never would. At that moment the doorbell rang, followed by a pounding on the perfectly painted autumn-rust door. Helen turned her glare toward the noise — there was no way she was going to answer it.

Sighing, Alison went to the front hall. The pounding continued.

"One second!" she yelled.

Then she looked through the peephole and saw what looked like the entire FBI outside, lights flashing.

Unleash the secrets within...

Meggie and her father Mo share a peaceful life together. But one evening a mysterious stranger forces Mo to reveal his extraordinary gift—a gift Meggie may also possess. Discover their remarkable secret—and how it changes their lives forever—in this thrilling adventure.